The
DEMENTIA CONSPIRACY

The DEMENTIA CONSPIRACY

A NOVEL

DAVID BARTLE WATTS
Licensed Private Investigator

MILL CITY PRESS

Mill City Press, Inc.
2301 Lucien Way #415
Maitland, FL 32751
407.339.4217
www.millcitypress.net

Printed in the United States of America

ISBN-13: 978-1-54564-861-2

This is a novel—a work of fiction. That said, the referenced cities, towns, and counties in New Jersey and New York and any physical features therein, such as streets, waterways and restaurants are real.

Several characters in this book are patterned after real people, as well.

"Mack" Mackey, the author's step-father-in-law, died in 1972. Although he was not an investigator while on this earth, he would approve of using his name as the "good guy" protagonist.

Bob and Brenda Higgins are real-life New Jersey private investigators. Kevin Murray is a licensed investigator, and a high-level security expert who specializes in electronic eavesdropping detection. Both have given permission for use of their identities.

All other names, characters, incidents and places are imaginary and any resemblance to actual persons, living or dead, or to actual events, is unintentional and coincidental.

Dedicated to Linda Rose

My wife, my life

Chapter *One*

Theodore "Ted" Archer worked alone. Depending on others had taught him hard lessons. On jobs like this one, missteps were out of the question.

He had followed Henry Lott each morning and after work for almost two weeks, patiently waiting. Patience was Archer's hallmark, an asset he picked up early in his career.

Henry was a creature of habit, so tailing him was easy. But Archer was troubled. Henry hadn't yet driven down a steep enough hill—nor rounded a sharp enough curve—dangerous enough to create a fatal "accident." Not yet.

Ted's phone buzzed. "Speak."

"Any progress?" Ted knew the voice.

"No, the jerk likes the flats and drives like a freaking nun. What can I say?" He hesitated, sighed and said, "Patience, doctor, patience." He dropped the call and shook his head in disgust. *Corporates have no concept of the real world. Within*

1

their bubbled existence, they get to play God, while I clean their dirty laundry.

Henry Lott parked his year-old Toyota Prius in his mother's driveway, oblivious to Archer's white Dodge minivan cruising down the street behind him. He took a deep breath, gazing up at the front of the house with its green shutters needing paint. He lived there too, but only temporarily. At least, that was the plan—a plan that had stretched into three years now. He dreaded these daily home-comings. *Mother will get on my case, as soon as I open the door.* Setting anxiety aside, he bucked up and reluctantly forced himself up the walk.

"Hey Mother, I'm home." As always, he yelled.

As always, she yelled back. "I know. I know. Come in here, I need to talk to you, Hankie."

Melanie Lott's hospital bed was set up in what had been her dining room. In her early 70s, Melanie's severe degenerative disc disease had taken over her existence. She was bitter. She crabbed at her Hankie whenever he was within range.

"I'm worried about your brother. He doesn't call or stop in to see me and you didn't call me today, either."

"Mark was just here last weekend, Mother. He has a job, you know, and so do I."

Sniffling, she continued, "And what's been bothering you lately? You never used to talk back to me."

The tears are real enough, but still part of the act, he mused. "I'm fine, Mother. Just those same old pressures at work. I'm fine."

Mother Lott whined on, "How many times did I tell you? You're not cut out for that big company. You go to school for pharmacy and you end up buried in a laboratory all day. It's not healthy." Peering over glasses teetering at the end of her nose—and with wrists furiously flicking knitting needles back and forth—she fired volley after volley. "I wish you had stuck with pharmacy, Hankie. You could have your own drugstore by now. But my wishes don't count for much, do they? Someday I'll be gone and you'll wish you listened to me."

Henry tuned her out. Her harping evaporated to background hum. His mind mulled over the month-long running-battle he'd been having with his lab manager at Analytic Bio-Pharm, the pharmaceutical lab where he worked.

His supervisor's persistent pressure was wearing on Henry. He couldn't sign off on the current protocol as being acceptable. Henry knew it wasn't ready and said so. He had

3

been stalling and arguing against rushing the project, but the supervisor, Wendy Hewitt, was not one to be refused. Not on her turf. *Every day, same thing. I should stand up to her more. She will get someone hurt if she makes me sign off.*

In their most recent go-round, she pushed hard.

"Now, you listen to me," Wendy said. "We have to move this along with no more delays. Animal testing is done. You've held this up way too long. This is safe, dammit, and you know how important it is. You're worrying over something that isn't there or doesn't matter. This project goes upstairs for human trials, and I mean right now."

Wendy had pointed a threatening finger at Henry, adding, "And you make sure your notes match up with the target we set, Henry. . . or else! Do you understand?" Wendy then slammed the lab door behind her as she left.

Henry understood. He understood that lab notes on 14168-ALZ in his own handwriting would be part of the submission to the FDA's Center for Drug Evaluation and Research. He understood rules required that everyone involved must be "on board" when clinical trials shift from animals to testing on humans. And he understood how important an effective new Alzheimer's drug could be in terms of lives and billions of dollars if it proved out.

14168-ALZ was a new type of investigational medication intended to target proteins in the brain and this study evaluated its effectiveness in slowing the progression of early-onset Alzheimer's Disease.

Henry surmised that ABP's new research director, Dr. Peter McGinn, was behind the pressure for fast-tracking 14168-ALZ. So far, testing had shown potential, but, as far as Henry was concerned, the data was not convincing enough to warrant human testing.

After 12 years working in bio-laboratories, Henry had seen conflict before between honest research and pressure to get a drug to market. His work put him in a position to verify or reject the efficacy of the drug being tested and 14168-ALZ wasn't making the grade. His not-so-subtle way of challenging what he believed was precipitous decision-making annoyed Wendy. He had hung a small sign over his work area that said, "Do you want it done right . . . or Tuesday?" Whenever nearby, Wendy glowered at that sign. She didn't like others posting statements in *her* lab.

And that wasn't all Henry understood. He knew Wendy Hewitt and Dr. McGinn were lovers—he came across them embracing in a stockroom, and they knew he knew. Ever since that awkward encounter, Wendy criticized everything Henry did. But his progress notes on the Alzheimer's drug, which Wendy wanted altered, were her major complaint.

Henry's concern was justified. His work had revealed that certain levels of proteins produced aberrant behavior in lab rats. Test subjects became agitated and sullen. Normally docile and accustomed to human handling, some rats became aggressive when the drug was administered. That spelled trouble for the project. Reporting it spelled trouble for Henry.

Normally, Henry was a compliant type of guy. He went along to get along. But not this time. He refused to sign off on Wendy's reformulated notes. He couldn't betray a part of himself that knew right from wrong. But in case the project went ahead without his findings—and, in his mind, as a kind of insurance—he hid his meticulously kept original data in the lab.

His mother's carping voice yanked him back into the present moment. His patience worn, Henry shouted, "Mother, just leave me alone, will ya? I've got a lot on my plate right now." He retreated to his study and sank into the recliner. *What should I do? How can I stop this madness? What if someone dies? Will it be my fault?*

Chapter *Two*

Two weeks earlier

Square-jawed, at **six-three and physically fit**, former Navy SEAL and DEA agent, Ted Archer did not suffer fools gladly. He had a tough guy reputation, having fought—and killed—in clandestine actions on behalf of the U.S. government from jungles to deserts worldwide.

Killing came easy to Archer. But he felt betrayed when he was reprimanded for doing the very thing he was trained to do: kill the enemy. The problem was Ted had a habit of going over the line. That is, he chose extreme violence at times when lesser measures would have sufficed. In time it caught up with him. The Navy furloughed him for disobeying orders prohibiting violence in a secret Libyan operation. His subsequent five-year stint in the DEA ended no better. He had no choice but to rein in his outside-the-box temperament and settle down. Settling down—but only for appearance's sake.

He transitioned to civilian life selling his uniquely malevolent services in the private sector to anyone needing "special" jobs.

In other words, Archer was a hired gun—a hit man. In certain circles his special skills were in demand. When tinhorn dictators needed scores settled or when politicians wanted leverage, Archer was a go-to-guy, he got results.

Lack of empathy was an attribute in his line of work. Archer excelled in that category. His victims were merely litter to be dispensed with during assignments—or as he called them: "operations." When corporations sought his unique skillset, Archer accommodated. He could play in that world, too. Archer thought, *Politics is politics: whether in the military, the business world, in politics itself.* He could be as erudite as the next guy if he had to be and he was also thorough, ruthless and unforgiving. Those three traits defined him at his core.

ABP's vice-president, Dr. Peter McGinn—no stranger to off-the-book transactions—needed "special" help. His whole career was on the line and it was increasingly clear that lab technician Henry Lott was in his way. This drug had the potential to rake in billions and take him to the top of the industry. No little do-gooder was going to stand in his way. He remembered some loose talk once by another corporate executive of similar and questionable morality. The exec had mentioned a scary guy who had roughed up one of his colleagues. Someone named Archer.

McGinn sat at his large Grand Palais executive desk across from Archer. Ornate French Provincial furniture complimented the cascading taupe drapes with gold-colored pull-chords. Rich, grey-paneled walls served as backdrop for Italian marble side tables. Facing the desk, four imported turquoise upholstered wing chairs were evenly spaced on the deep-grey Nourison carpet. Two office windows presented a bucolic view of a retention pond and ABP's meticulously maintained lawn and trees below.

"You come highly recommended, Mr. Archer." Like Archer, McGinn was thorough. He never put a foot down without knowing what was under it. He sat back and struck a condescending pose—chin up, looking down his nose—in an attempt to assert dominance.

As if he didn't already know the answer, he asked, "So, just what is it that you do?"

Archer had met McGinn's type before. He thought, A*nother corporate executive with an overblown opinion of himself. I'll play along.*

"I am a problem solver, Dr. McGinn. I get things fixed." He crossed his legs confidently and settled deeper into one of the wing chairs.

"Hmm . . . and just how do you go about getting things, as you say, 'fixed?'"

"Whatever it takes." Narrowing his eyes and leaning forward, he repeated, "Whatever. It. Takes!" Archer's inclination for making and holding eye contact often made people uncomfortable. McGinn was no exception.

"Ahem . . ." McGinn retreated from Archer's penetrating gaze. He repositioned himself and spoke earnestly, "Okay. Here's our problem."

McGinn's expression darkened. "We have a laboratory employee who won't play ball. He's kind of a weakling. Insecure, unstable. We can tell he's struggling with his conscience and we can't be sure which way he will go with it. My assistant has been trying everything possible to bring him around to approve moving things along by signing off on our project. She's threatened him and he doesn't even react. If he makes a bad decision on this and holds us up, it will set the company back immeasurably. Know the type?"

"I do." Archer thought a moment. "He's an unknown quantity in a circumstance where you can't afford one."

"You do understand. But allow me to provide additional perspective. This new drug has huge potential. It's bigger than anything. More important that one man. It will be worth hundreds of millions—probably billions—once we get it into production. I—we—simply cannot sit around and do nothing while this little fool threatens a tremendous medical breakthrough in Alzheimer's research. Drastic measures are called for."

"So, just exactly what is it you need done?" *He's having trouble getting it out. Just say it!*

McGinn sighed deeply and with feigned indifference calmly said, "We've thought it over. Warnings haven't worked, which is why you're here." His voice quivered a bit as he spewed it out. It was as if he was hearing someone else speak the incriminating words. "Too much is on the line. We want him gone. Out of the way. Removed. Whatever way you say it."

Taken aback by the magnitude of what he had just uttered, McGinn thought, *I don't believe I said it. I'm all in now.* He continued — sentimentality aside — and in a more business-like tone, "Of course, there should be nothing leading back to . . ."

"Of course." Archer waived it off. "Goes without saying."

Still uncomfortable, McGinn added, "And you should know, Mr. Archer, this decision was not reached casually. I mean, there's *so much* at stake here."

"I understand. I really do. You should know, I handle many problems of this nature. Sometimes, drastic measures are called for requiring a specialist. That's who I am and why I'm here."

McGinn stared at Archer for an awkward moment. He thought, *This stuff rolls right off his lips. Other than the obvious, it sounds like any business meeting, not a conspiracy for murder.* McGinn slid a small piece of paper across the desk. It contained Henry Lott's name, address, company photo and vehicle description.

"And here is a payment, Mr. Archer. You are now on retainer as a security consultant for ABP," as he pushed an envelope across his desk.

Archer saw right through the man. *This is all new to you. You don't have a clue of what you're getting yourself into. I know your type, Mr. Corporate.* He cautioned himself, though, *Stay on your toes, with this guy, Ted.*

Archer suggested, "You might want to include some other duties for me, too. That will give me cover for meeting with you here in the office." He opened the envelope, looked at the check and folded it into his shirt pocket. "This will do only as a retainer, Dr. McGinn but I expect twice that when the job is done." He looked into McGinn's eyes with a chilly stare, "Agreed?"

McGinn blinked, broke eye contact and conceded, "This is too important for me not to agree." He thought for a moment, then said, "Pardon the clumsy question: Are you computer literate? I mean as far as cybersecurity is concerned?"

"I'm comfortable with that. In my former positions, security—especially of the cyber nature—was an imperative" Ted chuckled to himself. *He has no idea how much cybersecurity, and insecurity, I am capable of. What a corporate asshole!*

"Then it's settled. You are our new cybersecurity expert. Welcome aboard, Mr. Archer." McGinn rose and extended his hand. Archer took it and squeezed back just a little more than necessary, sending a message: *You might be the head honcho around here, but you are not my master. My world is blunt force, not shady dealings by mealy-mouths. I own you now.*

From his office window, McGinn watched Archer walk to his car. He thought, *Tough guy. Smooth, but with a ruthless underside. He'll get it done.* His gaze drifted to Canadian geese skidding to splashy landings on the retention pond. *My life should be so simple!*

He watched ripples spread across the pond and reflected on his own position: At 56, he thought this was the last stop in his corporate career. He would make it big here or die trying. When he was offered the executive vice-presidency at ABP, he jumped at it. He was on his way out at his last company anyway; he bailed out after nearly getting caught taking a major kick-back on a building refurbishment.

McGinn planned to be president and CEO of ABP soon. All he had to do was move Alfred Stewart out. That would happen when the board of directors realized he personally brought 14168-ALZ from its beginnings as a scientific concept, right through to the marketplace. *No Boy Scout-type like Henry Lott is gonna stand in my way!*

Chapter *Three*

Julie Owens peeked over the top of Henry's cubicle with a friendly offer. "Coffee?"

They sat next to each other at the break room picnic table. Julie was sharp enough to pick up on what was going on and the pressure Henry was under with his dilemma. She spoke first. "Hank, you gotta do something. What if someone in the trial is hurt or dies?"

"I know, I know. I haven't been able to sleep, Julie. It's tearing me apart." Henry's hands were shaking. His face contorted, he added, "And if I sent a note anonymously to the FDA, McGinn and Wendy wouldn't have to think twice to come up with me." Shaking his head, he agonized, "I don't know how much more I can stomach from Wendy.

"It's not really her, Hank, it comes down from McGinn. But don't they realize how dangerous going forward could be? I mean people could die!"

Henry said, "I am not a troublemaker, Julie, but there are limits to how far I can be pushed."

She reached out and took his hand, "Hank, I know what kind of a person you are. You will do the right thing."

Unseen by Henry and Julie, Wendy Hewitt withdrew silently from the break room hallway and hustled toward ABP's executive offices. *Peter will want to know about this.*

Coffee cups emptied, Henry said, "Julie, we need to talk, and I mean away from here. Tomorrow is Saturday, a good day for a ride in the country and . . ." Henry stammered and finally blurted out, "I always wanted to ask you out, but never had the nerve." The pressure he had been under recently seemed to push his inhibitions aside.

Julie, also a timid soul, blushed and said, "That would be great. I was hoping you'd get around to it. Tomorrow sounds good. Pick me up around ten, okay?"

Henry raised his eyebrows and eagerly nodded, "Ten it is then." His confidence was buoyed. *Well, that wasn't as hard as I thought it would be.* Then, as always, self-doubt crept back in. *She's probably just feeling sorry for me.*

McGinn's text said it was urgent. Archer guided his white Dodge minivan up the long drive to the company parking lot. The drive along Route 206 to the Montgomery Township, New Jersey corporate offices of ABP was free of traffic by mid-morning. Princeton was just another 20 minutes south and Bridgewater a half-hour north. *A pleasant business setting in a rural area; yet close enough to population areas where employees could live,* he thought. He smirked. *Not a bad setting for corporate mischief, either.* Archer pushed aside the heavy glass door to ABP's entrance, keeping his appointment with Dr. McGinn.

At this, their second meeting, McGinn's frown made plain his impatience. "So, Mr. Archer, how is our little project coming along?" Senior vice president Dr. Peter McGinn was seated behind his desk, within the luxurious atmosphere of his executive office.

Archer thought, *Our little project? What a fool!* "As I explained, Dr. McGinn, conditions have to be just so to pull this off. I have handled similar assignments and pushing the envelope is dangerous. It must look like an accident. Neither of us needs or wants any connection to the outcome, right?"

"Oh, absolutely. You're right." McGinn was standing at the window, his back to Archer and speaking over his right shoulder. "But this is coming to a head. I have information that this guy is no longer on the fence. We think he's about to shoot his mouth off, become a whistle-blower. He's gone so far as to threaten contacting the Federal Drug Administration. That's serious shit, Mr. Archer. And the type of shit a pharma company like ours cannot abide."

"Are you sure? Sometimes things look worse than they really are. You know, one can overreact when things don't move along quickly enough."

McGinn, irritated with Archer's seemingly lackadaisical attitude, whipped around and exclaimed, "Do you think it might be significant that one of my trusted employees over-heard him discussing his options? *His* options, for Christ's sake, including the goddamn FDA! If that is allowed to hap. . ."

Archer interrupted with a raised hand, "Okay. Okay. Relax, Dr. McGinn, your problem will be solved soon." *Gotta watch you. You lack self-control. Reactive. Easily unhinged.*

McGinn was not completely satisfied with Archer's atti-tude. "Listen," he demanded. "Listen carefully, Mr. Archer. Up until now, you and I have had a sort of 'contractual' arrangement, if you will. I hired you to do a job, that's all. But things are rapidly changing. I am willing to offer you much, much more when you help me take control of this company.

This is a once in a lifetime opportunity. You get this done and you will be sitting pretty. That's a promise."

Archer smiled grimly, his response unambiguous. "Make me a promise you don't keep and you'll regret it."

Chapter *Four*

Archer's minivan trailed several cars behind the young couple as they weaved through wooded sections of Tewksbury Township along Old Turnpike Road. Lunch at the Brew Pub in Long Valley, with its relaxed, rustic atmosphere, eased conversation along between these two introverted spirits.

"You know, Julie, I've always had a hard time putting things into words. My thoughts get all bunched up in my head and don't seem to come out right. But not with you. I can talk to you." Henry reached over and squeezed Julie's hand.

"Thanks, Henry. I feel comfortable with you, too." Julie let her guard down with very few people, but Henry was different. *Different, but nice, too,* she thought, stealing a sideways glance. His driving was relaxed: one hand on the wheel, the other casually gripping the roof, his elbow poking out the open window. *He's at ease today. I think he's reached a decision.*

Finally, Henry broached the subject. "I don't see how I can sign off on the protocol using those doctored-up notes, but they're going to try every way they can to make me." He hesitated then confided in a conspiratorial tone, leaning toward her, almost whispering, "And I didn't destroy my original lab notes, I hid them. I'll show you Monday." He threw a quick wink at her and said, "Here's a puzzle for you to think about over the weekend. Those notes will be *food for thought*." He chuckled and drove on.

"Hmm." Julie giggled inwardly, *I like you, Henry Lott. I like you a lot!* They continued in silence along Old Turnpike Road, its open farmland offering splendid views on either side.

Archer's terrain-assessing, military-trained mind was in operational mode. During one of his "operations," he had worked with an experienced hacker whose main expertise was in vehicle technology. He learned enough to have the technical expertise to cause a crash, but he needed a steep hill or a sharp curve to set it up. He reached across and lit his lap top's screen with a light tap. Looking back up, an opportunity on the road seemed imminent. *Looking good. Getting close . . . Oh, yeah!*

A slow curve to the right appeared, then an immediate downhill sharp left-turn. Archer could always recognize potential. *You'd have to brake hard to make it around this one. I like this road. Here we go. Perfect! Do it now, Ted.*

With no other cars ahead of his target, Archer pressed ENTER. Preset entries flashed through a progression of computerized events. Internet commands flew. Archer couldn't resist wisecracking, "Three, two, one. Kaboom!"

Julie yelled, "Henry, why are we speeding up?" She screamed, her voice lost in the roar of sudden acceleration, "What's goin' on? Please! Oh my God, Henry. . ."

Wide-eyed, Henry fought hard. His shoulder muscles stiffened. He stood on the brakes. But neither steering nor brakes would budge. Shifting into passing gear, the Prius rocketed forward, its small high-pitched engine straining toward 75 miles per hour. Crashing through and over a metal barrier, its right side launched upward. Airborne with no hindrance, a right-to-left barrel roll triggered an upside-down landing in a meadow. Roof-skidding forward on wet grass without losing momentum, the careening Prius spewed mud and vegetation in all directions

Among the weeds were strewn several heavy 20 foot lengths of metal bracings left over during construction of overhead high-tension wires. One found the little Prius and pierced its windshield then rammed through Henry Lott's chest like a blunt spear, finally coming to a gouging-halt against the rear passenger backrest.

Then deafening silence.

Archer slowed, then stopped, joining other motorists gaping at the inverted, smoking wreck. Some climbed the guardrail and ran down into the gully to render aid. Others stood back on the roadway gawking, too terrified to approach, yet morbid curiosity gripping them like a perverse magnet.

An excited woman turned to Archer and said, "I've never seen anything like that before. That car just seemed to take off . . . for no reason. It was horrible."

"Yeah, it was bad. I was just behind you. Think anyone was killed?"

"Oh my. I'm afraid so. Had to be. It looks really bad."

Archer had "visited" scenes like this before. In fact, he had perfected the technique in South America with the help of another former DEA employee and computer wizard dubbed "The Flash."

Archer stepped back from the rubberneckers and left a text message, "Hey Flashy. It worked again. I owe ya."

Archer smiled, very pleased with himself. He had initially hoped to have access to Henry's car to physically hack into its OBD II port and its computer command center but could never find the opportunity. So, he went to Plan B. He ran the license plate to obtain the vehicle identification number to get what he needed. Archer knew that auto companies used VINs to identify each vehicle manufactured, along with all its components. The VIN was the key to wireless access, as well. That's all he needed.

Flash had put it this way: "There's so much code in a typical car from so many different vendors that it can be virtually impossible for auto makers to know all the software inside their vehicles. That's why they hire "white hat" hackers to find the bugs in their computer systems. It's possible to break into a car's command center without physically plugging into a port. We just have to find a hole somewhere within one of the networks to sneak in. From there, we can mess with just about anything."

Archer had done his homework. Using the Prius VIN and a schematic of its wiring and command system, he found a hole in its Bluetooth. It was what he was looking for and it worked, as it had for him once before.

Driving from the accident scene with first responders loudly approaching from the opposite direction, he sent a text to McGinn's personal cell phone.

"It's done."

Chapter *Five*

During the great depression in the 1930's, family patriarch Alfred S. Stewart, entrepreneur and bio-chemist, staked his claim in the fledgling bio-pharmaceutical field. His start-up company, Stewart Research, was situated in a shabby rented warehouse in Somerville, New Jersey with a laboratory at ground level and offices in the second-floor loft. There were many hardships getting started. Trained assistants were tough to find. Stewart had to conduct much of the research himself, resulting in long days and nights. Those early years—while not financially rewarding—established Stewart as a credible researcher. He took on projects subcontracted from larger pharmaceutical companies and was looked upon as hardworking, thorough, and above all, an honest businessman.

When World War II broke out, everything changed. The federal government recognized that more soldiers were put out of action by diseases such as influenza, bacterial meningitis, pneumonia, measles and mumps than by combat injuries.

Vaccines were desperately needed, especially in the Pacific and Italian combat theaters. So, as fortunes of war would have it, Stewart Research became a beneficiary of military necessity.

Alfred Stewart teamed with former clients and others in the field to develop many of the vaccines still in production today. The company's bank accounts swelled. Alfred Stewart learned the value of taking half-a-loaf as he cooperatively shared research and development with others, building success and good will. This business model and who he was as a person created a powerhouse company.

When Alfred's health began to falter, his eldest son, Alfred S. Stewart, Jr., took over the business. But the younger Stewart died suddenly of a stroke in 1982. Junior's only real contribution during his short seven-year tenure was a name change to Analytic Bio-Pharma. His rationale for the name change was to establish a more product-descriptive identity. This resulted in doing away with the family name the company had worn for decades. Nonetheless, the family succession continued. His own son, Alfred S. Stewart, III, a Princeton graduate, was bright and was old enough at 34 to step in and continue the work of his predecessors. Alfred III had tolerated his father, but revered his grandfather and loved the company. It was his life.

Alfred III was thrilled beyond words the day his executive vice-president told him of findings related to the "impressive" 14168-ALZ. And he filled with pride and excitement the day he announced his company's initial findings to the press. He pulled the microphone closer.

"Today we announce a wonderful breakthrough in the long fight against Alzheimer's Disease." Unlike his father and grandfather, this Stewart was at his best speaking before a group. "As we know, Alzheimer's Disease, the sixth leading cause of death in this country, is an insidious condition that robs patients of their very cognitive presence in the human community. In the next 25 years, between 10 and 15 million Americans will suffer from this disease. Unlike cancer and heart disease, there have been no major advances to speak of. Despite pouring billions of dollars into research, science has made negligible progress in its quest to conquer Alzheimer's.

Well, today I am pleased to say that has changed. Our scientists at Analytic Bio-Pharm have isolated a combination of proteins that have been shown to dramatically slow progression of the disease. While still in early trials, research looks very promising. We will keep you advised on a regular basis." Ending on an emotional level and in a tremulous voice he added, "And, in conclusion, I just have to say, today both my grandfather and father would be so proud of our company and its accomplishments. Thank you all for coming."

President Stewart stepped down from the podium, as those in the media rose from their chairs and began energetically milling about the large conference room. Most were on their cell phones dictating the huge news to their respective newspaper, radio and television outlets. Stewart turned to his executive vice-president, Dr. Peter McGinn, and grinned. "I think that went well, Peter."

"Yes, it did Alfred. Do you think they even realize how significant this is? And as far as the competition is concerned, you gave them enough data to keep them guessing, yet not enough to give away any secrets. Good job!" McGinn leaned closer, taking Stewart's elbow, and in a secretive tone said, "Along those same lines, I've just engaged a fellow who has some special expertise in security." They began walking down the long-carpeted hall heading toward their executive offices. "Last week you expressed concern about the competition getting into our britches. Do you recall that conversation? Corporate espionage and such?"

"Yes, yes, I remember. Good idea. . . the new hire, I mean. I'd like to meet him."

"He's already proven his worth. He has a certain flair for getting things done. The best part is he's an outside consultant, not on payroll."

"Smart, Peter, smart."

They continued their walk down the hall. McGinn marveled at how easy it was to manipulate his naïve boss. He watched as Stewart greeted his secretary and stepped smiling into his corner office. McGinn chatted up the secretary and watched through the door opening, as Stewart stood fixated on the portrait of his grandfather over the fireplace. McGinn thought, *Go ahead, old fool. Enjoy your melancholy reverie. You might be the figurehead around here for now, but I am the future of this outfit. Go to your dilettante parties. Play golf. Give speeches. Your days are numbered old man.*

Chapter *Six*

Sergeant **Rex Huntley walked around** Lott's Prius in the Tewksbury Township police impound yard. He took notes. *Extensive damage: Roof severely caved-in. Right front quarter crushed with wheel at an odd angle. Missing windshield. Steering wheel torn off its column. Raw holes ripped through both driver's side front and rear backrests.* Aloud, he said, "Gut-wrenching impact. Nasty! Nasty!"

Even though this wasn't Huntley's first auto fatality, there was always something about a bloody passenger compartment that fascinated. Dark bloody stains were splashed everywhere, but thickest on the driver's ceiling and backrest, where Henry Lott's body surrendered its precious essence.

Later, at the accident scene, Rex continued his investigation. He always felt a sense of humility in such moments. A hard-nosed detective, he also had a human side, too. *It was here that someone died,* he reflected. In a way, it seemed he was standing on sacred ground. *Were it not for the element of luck and time, this could've been me.* He shook it off, his detached professional composure returning. *I wonder what happened in the final seconds? A* blood-stained metal brace lay on matted-down grass. Rex kicked it. *You must've been poised at just the right angle. Tough break.* He stepped over the discarded bandage wrappings strewn about the scene. They told their own story.

He pictured the accident dynamic. *Let's see. Witnesses said the car was going along normally, then took off like a missile, straight into and over the guardrail and flipped.* Using his left hand, he "drove" the vehicle's path leading up to impact, twisting to palm-up and flipping over. Again, he couldn't help it: a more personal observation crept into his impassive investigator mindset. *Whew, I can't imagine how it must have been for those first responders seeing the guy and getting that hunk of metal separated from his body. Ugh! I'll never get used to this.*

Huntley's concentration was broken by someone approaching. "Hey Sarge, how ya doin'?" Hunterdon County Prosecutor Detective John Cassini held a clipboard with his left hand and shook Huntley's with his right.

"Bad one, huh?"

Huntley slowly nodded his head. "After you take a look, let's take a ride to the medical center and see if our passenger is able to talk yet."

"I heard she was banged up pretty bad."

"Yeah. Multiple fractures, including a head injury. Doctors said the first hours it was touch and go, but I just learned she'll pull through." As he stepped away, Huntley looked back at the disturbed ground and commented, "Hopefully, she can help us figure out what happened here."

Julie Owens was in intensive care and hooked up to several monitors. When the two men approached, she turned away. Her head was completely bandaged, with only her deeply scratched and stitched-up face showing. Her right eye was bruised and still closed. Her left arm was suspended in a cast. A drain tube came from beneath the covers.

Huntley and Cassini stood at the foot of the bed. "Ms. Owens, we're investigating the accident. Are you up for a couple of questions?" *It's always tough to put victims through this,* thought Huntley, *but necessary.* "We're sorry to disturb you, but I'm sure you want us get to the bottom of this."

Julie blankly looked at them, blinked, and seemed to be trying to focus. She spoke in a quiet, labored voice. "I don't remember much. Henry was driving, I know that. I remember screaming . . . then nothing." With that, she became agitated, "That's all I remember." She started crying, which brought about coughing and spasms. She flailed about. Monitors chirped. A nurse rushed in and tried to calm her, fussing with her patient's intravenous flow. With a dirty look at the detectives, and a dismissive jerking thumb, she needed only one word: "Out!"

Ambling down brightly lit antiseptic hallways, Cassini opined, "We really need an accident reconstructionist to go over the car and scene, Rex."

"Yeah. I'll put in a call to the state police. They eventually get around to reviewing all fatal accidents, but maybe I can get them onboard early." Rex was perplexed, too. "It is puzzling, isn't it? I mean, what would cause sudden acceleration like that? Driver distraction? Vehicle failure? Christ, it might even be suicide."

"Too bad she wasn't much help. Maybe later on."

Ted Archer sat behind an opened newspaper about 40 feet from Julie's room. As the detectives passed, he overheard Cassini's last comment and a little smile curled up on the side of his mouth.

Chapter *Seven*

Not even **12 miles from the headquarters** of Analytic Bio-Pharm another drama was unfolding. Sofia Rodriguez had been confused lately and her son, Jose, couldn't believe how his mother had changed. She was forgetful and spoke in jumbled sentences. This morning she said, "Jose, bring me the wash wagon. I have to catch up with the dog."

"Mama, what are you saying?" It pained Jose to see his mother so befuddled. His older sister, Maria, tried to explain it to Jose, but he wasn't having any of it.

"She does *not* have dementia. You just think that because you are a nurse and see sickness everywhere. She'll be okay. It's probably her nerves." Seeking some basis for his mother's mental state, he added, "And she gets this way every time she visits Uncle Diego. She shouldn't go there anymore."

Maria persisted, "You don't want to think it, Jose, so you don't see it. She's becoming more and more confused; she couldn't even remember my name yesterday."

Finally, Jose relented and the next afternoon they took their mother to visit a doctor referred by Maria's clinic supervisor. Dr. Barnes was a geriatrician, specializing in early on-set Alzheimer's Disease.

Following initial testing, he explained, "Your mother is in the first stages of dementia. She will likely be diagnosed with Alzheimer's before long. Frankly, there's not a lot that can be done. It gradually takes hold and people need more assistance with everyday things. There are some drugs that claim to slow the disease's progression, but I haven't seen that happen very often. Your love and patience will do more than anything I can prescribe." Tears welled in Sofia's eyes. Dr. Barnes sympathetically added, "Sorry. I wish I could be more helpful."

Perturbed with the hopelessness of what he'd just heard, Jose groaned, "But we can't do nothing. We have to help her somehow!"

Barnes frowned thoughtfully and turned to his lap top. "There is a new drug being tested that, according to researchers, is supposed to slow disease progression." He poked at the keyboard. His eyes brightened. "This is new. It says here that human trials are starting now and they are looking for patients with symptoms your mother exhibits."

His expression hopeful, he turned back to the young siblings. "Should I try and get her in?"

Jose wasn't so sure. "She's not a guinea pig. She's our mama."

Maria, the licensed practical nurse—more in tune with medical decisions—jumped at the chance. "Jose, it's our only hope. We have to do this. You're right, we cannot do nothing."

Jose conceded, "Okay, but not without Uncle Diego's blessing. Since Poppa died, he's head of the family and he is mama's brother. If he says it's okay, I'll go along."

Drawing Jose away from the doctor, Maria whispered, "You want a jailed, convicted criminal—a big-time drug dealer—to determine your mama's future? What's wrong with you?"

"Are you willing to do this without his permission?" Jose skeptically tilted his head and searched his sister's face.

"Hmm. . . I see what you mean. Then you go and talk to him this weekend, not me. He may be my uncle, but he scares me."

Jose sat at the thick visitor's glass waiting for Uncle Diego to emerge from within the bowels of New Jersey's state prison in Rahway, New Jersey. Jose looked around uncomfortably at other visitors engaged in conversation with inmates through an intercom system. He'd been here before, but always with his mother. He didn't like the place.

Diego Gomez sauntered over and sat on his side of the glass barrier. "Where's my sister, su madre?" He spoke quietly. Always alert, he skewed his head slightly, awaiting Jose's response.

Diego was not a big man, but his self-assurance more than made up for his slight stature. He had a tough, purposeful look about him. The look that let you know immediately he was someone you wouldn't want to mess with.

Street-wise and brutal when he needed to be, Diego survived his teenage years on the streets and back alleys of Medellin, Colombia. His cunning and vicious nature fueled a meteoric rise within the criminal underworld. But those same "attributes" targeted him as a drug king-pin within law enforcement circles. In his mind, being incarcerated was only a temporary inconvenience, a thing to be endured.

"So, answer the question, pequeño. Where is she?"

"She is why I am here. We have a problem."

Diego frowned, and to Jose's surprise, asked, "Is it her confusion? The last few times here, she acted, I don't know, different."

Relieved and glad he didn't have to raise the subject first with his uncle, Jose looked down and sadly nodded his head.

"Okay. What is it? Speak up."

"Mother is in a bad way. She has dementia. The doctor says there's no cure and she will only get worse. In time, she won't know us. Maria and I took her to a special doctor. . ."

Diego, broke in, his impatience brimming, "This is America. There's always a cure." He gritted his teeth, then took a moment to calm himself. "So, what did the special doctor say?"

"Uncle, I am not sure about doing this. Maria has convinced me there's no other way. With your permission, we are going to put her into a new research project with a drug company that says it has discovered something that could help her." Jose looked pleadingly at Diego. "It's called a drug trial. Maybe Maria's right." Jose's indecision was agonizingly obvious. "I hate to see this happening to our mama!"

Ignoring the boy's weakness, Diego answered right back, "Your sister is right. Do it." He raised himself and before turning to leave, asked, "What is the name of this drug company? They better be good!"

Chapter *Eight*

In his second floor office on East Main Street, Westfield, New Jersey, attorney Avery Reddy leaned back in his chair and studied the young man before him. Mark Lott seemed like a reasonable and rational person. He'd made an appointment to discuss an auto accident in which his older brother was killed a month previous. Reddy had already ordered a copy of the preliminary police report, so he knew what to expect in terms of basics: accident scene location; direction of travel; driver and passenger identification; date, time etc. But he was not prepared for an allegation of murder.

"Mr. Reddy, I know—I mean, I knew—my brother. He was not a fast driver. In fact, his dawdling in traffic drove me and everyone else crazy. There's no way he was 'speeding and lost control' like the police report said. There's more to this and I hope you don't think I am a conspiracy nut. Henry worked for a bio-pharmaceutical company and something was going on. He told me he couldn't say much about it, but he said things weren't right and he had to do something. I think he was about to become a whistle blower. I'm sure this was not an accident, Mr. Reddy, but I can't get anyone to look into it."

Reddy, a long-time trial attorney listened to the young man's earnest account of events and thought there might be something more to this accident. Even the wording in the police report was couched in vague terms. Some of the phraseology employed was unlike the "just the facts, ma'am" formula normally used in law enforcement: "unknown causation," "inexplicable acceleration," "no known history of depression," and "requires more in-depth examination." Use of these terms troubled Reddy and started him thinking things didn't add up.

The kid was clearly upset by his brother's death and Reddy was a compassionate guy. He listened intently. If he could be convinced there was enough substance to Mark's allegation, he would take the case.

"You are insinuating that his employer might have had him killed?"

"No, not insinuating. Oh, I don't know for sure, but I think so. I have no real proof. That's why I'm here. And I know it sounds far-fetched, but don't just believe me, Mr. Reddy. I left someone in your outer office who knows a lot more than I do. Mark rose and walked over to the door and signaled for Julie to come in. Over his shoulder, he continued, "That is, if and when she remembers."

Julie entered, her left arm still in a cast. Reddy stood up. Stitches removed from her face left ugly scars and hair had begun to grow back over the indentation on the top of her head. She gingerly lowered herself onto a side chair. Reddy could see there was a beautiful young girl beneath those injuries. He was struck by her grim appearance.

"This is Julie Owens. She worked with Henry and was his passenger when. . ."

"It's okay, Mark. I can explain for the lawyer." Though still in pain, Julie looked directly into Reddy's eyes and in a strong, firm voice said, "It's simple. They killed him. I know they did."

Julie described the pressure put upon Henry to alter his lab notes on 14168-ALZ by his supervisor at ABP and his coming to grips with becoming a whistleblower. She told Reddy how Henry's research findings were rejected in the company's rush to move the trial into human testing, and that he refused to sign off on it.

"He drove like an old lady. There's no way Henry was negligent. He never would have sped up like that. It must have been the car. Something was done to it. I don't know what, but it wasn't right. It just took off." She took a deep breath, trying to keep her composure. "I only wish I was clear on everything that happened that day. I'm still so fuzzy." She paused to gather her thoughts and said, "Mr. Reddy, Henry was no hero. He was just a guy, but a good guy and he really cared about what would happen to people if that drug was ever marketed without proper testing. That makes him a hero to me." A tear formed as she shifted her weight, discomfort—both physical and emotional—palpable. Reddy grimaced sympathetically.

Reddy probed, "Can you tell me exactly what happened in the moments before the car sped up?"

Julie replied, "I only wish I could. Somehow, that's blacked out. I've tried, but I can't remember. All I remember is the car flying forward and I was screaming and yelling, 'Henry!'" Her far away frown implied she was momentarily in another dimension—straining, searching. Conversation was awkwardly on hold. Attorney Reddy and Mark exchanged an uncomfortable glance.

Mark broke the silence. "The fatal 'accident' report by the police expert isn't out yet, but I had a talk with state police investigators. They couldn't find anything wrong with the steering or brakes. Law enforcement considers this a closed case. They say, 'He was speeding and lost control.' It just looks like they want to move on. I guess they don't have anything else to hang their hat on." He looked at Julie, back at Reddy and said, "It's not a closed case with us. We need someone to look closer and we want you to help us. Please."

Attorney Reddy signaled a pause and tapped the office intercom. "Janice, please get me Mack. If he's not in, ask Nezzie to page him. Important."

A moment later private investigator "Mack" Mackey was on the line with Reddy. "Mack, I have clients in my office needing your services. When can you get in here?"

Reddy nodded and said, "Good. See you then." He turned to Mark and Julie saying, "The best investigator is what you need, and I have him coming in later. He said he could be here by four o'clock today. Can you come back then?"

"We can, Mr. Reddy, but we haven't discussed your fee and I'm not sure we can afford an investigator," Mark said. Julie looked from Mark to Reddy in anticipation.

"I don't want to get your hopes up, but if what you've been telling me turns out to be true, fees will not be a problem. This case could pay for itself if it checks out. I'm not going to charge you until my man, Mack, has a chance to look into this. If I take the case, any fee will come out of a judgment or settlement." As an afterthought, he threw in, "And you both could come out of this set for life, if what you're telling me is true. For now, let's take things one at a time."

"Pleasure to meet you. Sorry about your loss." Mack greeted Reddy's new clients in the conference room. As they all sat down, Mack, in an effort to break the ice, quipped, "You know, I always tease Mr. Reddy about all these books. Do lawyers really read them or are they just for show?"

Claude Frederick "Mack" Mackey, a former police detective, was in his 18th year as a New Jersey licensed private investigator. His six-foot frame and trim physical condition belied the balding head and crow's feet starting around his eyes. At 52, he was at the top of his game and his clients—mostly insurance companies, lawyers, and big corporations—respected his investigative abilities.

Not to be outdone, and with a sour face, Reddy said, "Pay no attention to him. He may be a good investigator, but he can be a pain in the neck sometimes."

Niceties aside, Mack listened while Reddy and his clients brought him up to speed. Mack asked a few questions and made notes. He came up with an initial plan of attack.

"First, what we need to do is conduct a really thorough examination of the Prius. Today's vehicles are complicated, and it wouldn't be hard to miss something. Not that the state police aren't competent. They surely are. But it would be worth it to put a second set of eyes on it. Don't you think so, Avery?"

Reddy agreed. "Mack, I can set us up with the expert witness I used in a case we won last year. He's in South Jersey, but he'll come up if I ask him to." He turned to Mark. "When you sent me the initial police report, I called Tewksbury Township police headquarters and requested they preserve the car, so that's taken care of."

Mack had another thought and directed it to Avery. "As to motive, if we had Henry's actual lab notes, we could examine them to see if they conflict with the data the company has put forward. That could constitute motive."

Reddy considered it for a moment. "Maybe so. It would depend on the degree of contradiction between Henry's and any fabricated data and how that relates to any effects or outcome. That would also call for an expert's opinion; but, yes, I think so." Reddy directed a question to Julie. "Can you think where Henry's notes might be?"

Julie hung her head and said, "Unfortunately, I have no idea where they are. I'm so sorry. I wish I could remember what Henry said before we crashed. I know he said something. Maybe it was about the notes; but it's not coming to me."

Mack wrapped it up. "If the facts are as you say, we are in for an uphill climb against a well-heeled corporation with deep pockets and a lot to lose. It's going to be a rough go, but Avery and I have been there before. I, for one, believe you may have something. But there's a lot to check out. I need to do some digging before we meet again."

Alone and able to talk more freely, the legal professionals went over the case again, each making suggestions toward a game plan from his own perspective: the investigator suggesting routes of inquiry, the lawyer citing legal possibilities. Even though they had worked together as a team on many cases over the years, this one had them more than a bit excited.

The hunt was on.

Chapter *Nine*

Maria Rodriguez and her mother, Sofia, sat in the waiting room of Somerset Hospital's Geriatric Studies Department. Arriving early for their 10:15 a.m. appointment, they had a chance to acclimate and look around at a roomful of other patients and family members. Maria spoke with a man to her left.

"I see you are here with your mother, too. Do you know anything more about the drug trial? I mean, how does it work?"

"My doctor told me Phase I usually takes a couple of months and everyone is monitored closely. There will be about 45 test subjects involved and we have to keep a log at home—of everything."

"You mean like changes in mood and stuff like that?"

"Uh huh, but they'll tell you all about it. I called ahead and asked a few questions. We'll have a check list to fill out every day. It has all kinds of things to watch for and there's a 24-hour emergency number to call with any questions we have. It's pretty well thought out, if you ask me. And the best part is the patient gets paid for participating—not a lot, but, hey, that helps, too."

A young man carrying a clipboard appeared from the "Employees Only" door. Patients and family members perked up in anticipation.

"Good morning. My name is Roy Evenson and I am a physician's assistant assigned to your drug trial. You all are here this morning because you have pre-qualified for Phase I of a medication being tested for its value in treating early-stage dementia. I am handing out initial information sheets that should answer most questions but let me go over some essential facts."

Evenson went on to explain the mechanics of administering the drug, along with patient trial-partner duties.

Sofia turned to Maria and whispered, "Does this mean I will be able to remember to turn off the stove?"

Maria took her hand, leaned over, quietly kissed her cheek and winked.

Discretion was essential, especially during working hours. Dr. McGinn and Wendy Hewitt left the Princeton Country Lodge in separate cars, arriving back at the company parking lot at about the same time. Upon walking through the employee entrance, they greeted each other cordially, as if for the first time today, prattling on about one work topic or another. But, Gus, the security guard—having picked up on their liaisons—chuckled as they walked past his post. He thought, *You two don't have to make up stuff for my benefit. I caught on a long time ago.*

A note on McGinn's desk summoned him to Alfred Stewart's office. Stewart's secretary, usually sociable, didn't make eye contact. She merely waived McGinn toward Stewart's closed office door, affecting diligence to paperwork on her desk. McGinn sensed something unusual was up.

"Good afternoon, Alfred. You wanted to see me?"

"Peter, you never told me one of our employees was killed in a terrible car accident."

McGinn started to speak, "Well. . ."

"You also never told me his passenger was another of our employees and that she was hurt badly."

"Alfred, I didn't want to trouble you. I consider it my job to handle these things and not burden you with minutiae."

Stewart's head jerked backward, his facial expression darkened. Anger building, he rose and thundered, "Minutiae? Really? That's not minutiae. You know how my family has always treated our employees. This is not acceptable, Peter." Stewart stood stiffly-erect, his hands clasped tightly behind his back, his jaw clenched. He took a deep breath to calm himself before speaking in a controlled but resolute voice.

"I want you to reach out to the families and see what we can do for them. And, Peter, I mean *you* personally. Understand?" Before McGinn could respond, the older man counseled, "Peter, I've watched you. You're good at what you do, but you need to work more on the human aspect of leadership. This isn't only about corporate profits and personal gain. Our employees are our company's lifeblood. We take care of them, they take care of us. Think about that."

McGinn, realizing he had overstepped and used insensitive language, back pedaled. "Alfred, of course, you are right. I didn't intend to sound callous. I will see to it immediately."

As he retreated from Stewart's office, he wondered, *how do I go about this? Maybe a family visit to the Lotts and the Owens girl should cover it. I'll check with HR, they probably have some kind of death benefit.* As an afterthought, he couldn't help admiring Stewart's intensity. *Wow, Alfred.*

Didn't know ya had it in ya. You might not be that easy to unseat, after all."

Mark Lott and Julie Owens sat waiting in the Lott family living room. "This oughta be good," said Mark. "And thanks for coming over on short notice. Having you here will catch him off guard, which is what we want."

Julie shook her head slowly, "It's about time somebody from the company showed up. How can people be so uncaring?"

Mark got up quickly and went to the window when he heard McGinn's Volvo arriving. He turned and took three strides back and turned on a tape recorder hidden on the bookcase. Mark whispered, "Remember, Julie, we have to keep our cool. This is important." She responded with a thumbs-up.

Chapter *Ten*

Mack phoned Avery Reddy as he drove back toward his office on Route 22 in Greenbrook, New Jersey. On speaker, he asked, "Avery, have you told Ms. Owens she has a case against Henry Lott's auto insurance policy? After all, a passenger has no liability, so she should have her medical bills paid and would be entitled to a pretty nice payday, considering how badly she was banged up."

"Yes. I did send a letter off to Lott's insurance carrier to determine policy limits and to put them on notice." Avery explained, "Julie's own personal injury protection coverage will take care of her medical bills. But you're right. As a passenger, she has a helluva law suit against Henry's liability policy. But if all this other stuff pans out, real money will come from the pharmaceutical company. And I mean *real* money."

"Yeah, that's what I was thinking." Mack paused and said, "Avery, I want to bring Bob Higgins in on this if you don't mind. He has those state police connections and comes up with good ideas. Besides, this is the kind of case that needs a sounding board close at hand."

"Okay, but put a muzzle on his lawyer jokes, will ya?"

"Oh, I dunno. He keeps everybody grounded with his bad jokes. His kiddin' around eases tension just when we need it."

"Humph!"

"Now that you've read what we have, so far, Bob, whaddaya think?"

Mack and Bob were talking over a beer at Ono Rosa restaurant in Bunnvale, about half-way between their two offices. "The O.R.," a friendly neighborhood bar serving mainly Italian cuisine, had a clientele of regulars who bantered back and forth, creating a pleasant atmosphere. Mack and Bob liked meeting there.

Bob wisecracked, "Did you hear about the restaurant on the moon? Great food, no atmosphere."

"Okay, comedian, let's get down to business. Here's the way I see it: On paper, it looks like he was speeding, lost control, went bottoms up and killed himself. That's the cop get-it-done-get-it-out version. I think there's more to it."

Bob answered thoughtfully, "So do I."

"Yeah, and I'm glad you agree. If you'd met with the dead kid's brother and his young female passenger as I did, you'd be even more convinced there's something goin' on here. Let's do pro and con. You go pro, Bob, and I'll go con. You first."

"Okay, off the cuff, here goes: First, there's no reasonable explanation why a driver would speed up on that curve. If he wanted to kill himself, he could've chosen a better place—like a big tree—and he probably wouldn't have taken a passenger with him. And just because there was a physical examination of the car, doesn't mean there's something we don't know about yet. I checked. There aren't any recalls for the Prius, so that's a dead end."

Bob thought another moment, then finally offered, "Hey, just because the two clients claim the company was behind it, doesn't mean it couldn't be true. Stranger things have happened. Besides, they don't come out of left field with it; they back it up with reasoning: Henry, according to them, may have been about to blow the whistle which would set back ABP a billion dollars in R and D. Maybe end the program. Couldn't that be enough to take action against Henry? After all, there would be many more billions in them-there pharmaceutical pills if they got to market. This is huge." Bob nodded his head and said, "I think it's plausible. Your turn.

"Okay, pal, an opposing view: Anyone's accelerator can get stuck to the floor, or he wasn't paying attention, or was reaching for something, or texting, or any everyday thing like that. He was speeding, like the report says, and lost control. It happens. As to the allegations against his employer: Aw, c'mon! What corporate executive has the stones for murder? It just doesn't hold water. The clients are upset having lost a brother and a boyfriend. Who wouldn't be? But why would we believe anything so bizarre as murder to save a possible dementia drug?"

Mack and Bob had investigated all kinds of cases together. They were friends and often bounced theories around. It kept them focused. Bob Higgins, a retired New Jersey State Police sergeant, survived more than his share of the murky side of human experience while "on the job," such as murder, rape, robberies and various other mayhem. Not much surprised him.

Mack summed it up. "Let's keep both arguments in mind as we go forward with this. I think first we should get back with Mark or Julie and identify someone in the company we should interview. Just to do a little cage-rattling. Ya think?"

"Oh yeah. Let's shake things up a little. Never know what could fall out."

The restaurant's amiable owner, known affectionately as "Uncle Tony," came over to their side of the bar and said, "Welcome to the O.R., gentlemen. Can I do a refill?" Always with the witty one-liners, he said, "You'll have to excuse my neglect, it's my first day on the job."

Mack leaned toward Bob, "He's been saying that the last 33 years."

"Nice place, though. Brenda makes me eat safe. I always use condiments." Bob grinned at Uncle Tony, "I'd order a water, but I don't want my liver to think it was donated to someone else."

Tony rolled his eyes and shook his head. He turned toward another customer and joked, "Ay, easy on the parmesan. That stuff costs 16 bucks a pound!"

Later that night, at his condo in North Plainfield, Mack and his live-in girlfriend, Penny, were sharing a pizza from Mr. Assante's, farther down Route 22. "Pen, what do you know about drug trials? I mean, just how tough is it to bring a new drug to market?

Penny Lund's condo had been conveniently just down the hall, but it seemed silly to keep both, considering how their relationship had grown. So, she sold hers and moved in with Mack. An emergency room nurse at Morristown Memorial Hospital, Penny worked rotating shifts. Considering the odd hours Mack kept in the private investigation business, any quiet time spent together was precious.

Mack's wife, Margie, died several years before. It was Penny who rescued him from an all-consuming depression. She wouldn't put up with negativity or "crappy melancholy," as she put it. Her gentle yet persistent cajoling eventually brought Mack around. There was an age difference: she in her late thirties, he in his early fifties; but it didn't play into their relationship. Mack referred to Penny as "my bubbly, freckle-faced cutie." They got along well, but marriage had not yet entered the conversation, she having just come off a painful divorce. It was a pleasure to share a quiet meal at home for once. Penny reached for another slice of pizza and took up Mack's question.

"The one thing I know for sure is that it's really tough and really expensive to get a drug through all the FDA obstacles.

You'd better have a lot of money, time, expertise and perseverance to get to the finish line. This is why so many pharma companies are sharing different aspects of research on the same project"

Penny thought a moment, then went on, "First, there's the *in-vitro* testing. Test tube stuff. Then it goes to *in-vivo*, animal testing. Before it gets to real, live human testing, a lot of scientists and research-types have reviewed and authenticated the results. If I remember right, there are four levels of human trials, too, each one tougher than the other. It's a long hard road to bring a drug to the public. And that's a good thing. I inject or medicate a lot of patients, and I often think about how important it is that pharma get it right. Why do you ask?"

"I'm working on a case that might involve drug testing notes and such. I'll probably need your help interpreting some of the technical stuff. Okay with you?"

"Sure, bring it on. I hope I can remember all my chemistry lab classes. Now, how about cracking another Coors Light over there, big boy?"

Chapter *Eleven*

iego Gomez didn't call his family often, but his sister's condition had him worried. "Jose, tell me. How is this drug trial coming along? No one has been to see me in two weeks. What's goin' on with my sister?"

"Uncle, I don't know what to do. Mama's not getting better. The guy at the hospital says we have to have patience, because the drug trial is only in its third week. But things are worse. You know what a kind and nice person mama is. Well, now she gets angry all the time. Instead of being confused, she loses her temper. She threw my breakfast at me this morning! I wonder if we made a mistake."

"What does your sister say?"

"Maria says we have to trust the medical people. I love her; but she is one of them, you know? She says this is just a side effect, but I don't like the changes goin' on."

Diego didn't speak. He and Sofia were close as children, she was the only one who looked out for him. She was the only one who stuck up for him when he got in trouble. News of her deteriorating condition put him in a deeply sad state. He stared at the bare wall above the prison pay phone. He pictured Sofia when they were eight and ten making sand castles on the beach at San Onofre back in Columbia.

Setting reverie aside, Diego said, "I think for now, we have to listen to your sister. She knows more about this than we do, Ask her to visit me."

One week later

"Why are you here? I told you I wanted to see Maria."

Jose smiled uncomfortably and said, "Maria is afraid of you." He put his head down and quietly added, "And she doesn't want to be seen here."

Diego's eyes drifted to the ceiling. He sighed. "Dios mio! She's ashamed of me." He leaned closer to the glass separating them. "How about you, Jose? Are you afraid of me? Are you ashamed, too?"

"Uncle, when my padre died, you became head of the family. I respect that. I accept that . . . nothing more. It is not for me to judge you. My only interest is my mother,"

"Smart kid."

Jose's frustration showed on his face. *It's not about you. It's about my mother!* "Uncle, what do we do now? Mama is not getting better after three weeks of this new treatment. They stick this IV thing in her arm and send her home after a couple hours of sitting there. Maria keeps notes on a clipboard." Jose was deflated. "It all seems so useless. Mama is getting worse and her anger . . . that scares me. What should we do?"

"What is the name of this hospital and drug company. I wanna check 'em out."

"You can do that in here?"

Diego laughed. "You're a nice kid, but you have a lot to learn."

McGinn was frustrated. "How do you know she won't take up where Lott left off when she recovers? She probably knows what he knew. She worked right next to him in the lab." McGinn clicked off speaker phone, "They were friends. Maybe more than friends."

Archer wasn't used to explaining himself in this detail, but he knew McGinn was the type that could become unhinged given the right circumstances. *I guess I have to hold this guy's hand.*

"Listen, all I know at this moment is the cops haven't gotten anything out of her at the hospital. I got lucky and overheard some of their conversation. She's messed up pretty good. She's blocked out the accident and probably hasn't mentioned anything about any problems at work, either."

"But can we really take that chance? Maybe we should do something about her, too."

Archer almost lost control of the van. "Not on the phone, you idiot!"

"Okay, okay. Come to the office as soon as you can."

Archer shook his head in disgust, as he drove up to the gate to his storage area and punched in the code to raise the barrier. Two aisles down he turned right and pulled up to the double-wide garage he rented. He remembered his first impression of this, his "Base Camp Alpha." *New Brunswick is a good place for my HQ. Centrally located with quick access to the turnpike and parkway, and not that far from New York or Philly with their international airports. The perfect set up.*

He stowed the van on the left side and, true to his security-conscious nature, scanned the outside area before pulling down the overhead door. He turned to his workshop in the adjoining garage area and sat at the oak-top workbench. Along the opposite wall were three plastic racks, each with five shelves, stockpiling what he called his "toys of the trade."

Archer's equipment outfitted any type of operation: pinhole and other covert video cameras, computer network penetration software, wiretap equipment, a TSCM (technical surveillance countermeasures) kit—used to protect himself against eavesdropping bugs, taps and cover video cameras—VoIP telephone wiretap apparatus, magnet-attached GPS trackers, police scanners, remote sensors and his favorite, a portable Stingray unit to monitor all cell phones in the area. He could use the Stingray in the van, as well. His assortment of weaponry included handguns, rifles and combat knives, a bullet-proof vest and a night-vision headset, all stored in a locked trunk on the floor. Never short of identities should they be needed, he also kept a stack of fake driver's licenses and passports in the trunk.

Ted Archer thought of himself as a one-man traveling, alphabetized wrecking crew: CIA, DEA, FBI, etc. Of course, he had "liberated" all this expensive paraphernalia over the years during his government assignments. His logic was, *Hey, I earned it by putting my butt on the line. Uncle Sam used me up and threw me out, and this boy ain't goin' away empty-handed.*

The first thing Archer did after renting the units was to tap into the storage area's electrical circuits for power and lighting, which also kept a fridge in the corner running and stocked with cold beer. He stayed late one night and installed a miniature satellite dish on the roof, so small it couldn't be seen from the ground. He paused to look around at his creation. *My man cave; I love it.*

Archer closed up and walked over to his black Infiniti Q70 parked behind a large RV inside the fence line. He banged around in his van when on the job; but the Q70 satisfied his need for the creature comforts he had missed all those years when roughing it on clandestine missions. Easing back into the comfy seat, he revved up the Q70 and headed toward his next meeting with McGinn. *Let's see what's on the creep's mind this time.*

Chapter *Twelve*

Investigator Bob Higgins was thinking back about the last thing Mack said to him, "Bob, I spoke to Julie Owens to get more detail on what was bothering Henry Lott. She mentioned a Wendy Hewitt, Henry's immediate boss, as being a problem. I'll be questioning her, but for now, I would like you to check out the company and what might be going on that's out of the ordinary. Let's take a week or so keeping an eye out in the parking lot and see what kicks up until we get the lay of the land and know more about the players. Right now, we're best off laying low and just observing."

After six days in the parking lot, Bob was getting restless and bored. *This is a long time to be sitting here and waiting ...for what?* He kept a log of employees' arrival and departure times, including taking down license plate numbers. However, when two people left in separate cars around 1:15 p.m. on Tuesday and Friday, then returned two hours later— ten minutes apart both days—Bob thought he might finally have something of interest. When it happened a third time, he followed the woman.

Wendy Hewitt parked in the back of the Princeton Country Lodge, quickly covering the several yards to the back door with her head down. Higgins pulled into the lot just in time to see her disappear down a hallway through the glass door.

Well, whaddaya know! The Hewitt Honda was parked just two spaces away from the McGinn Volvo. *Mack was right, "It doesn't stink until you stir it." A little hanky-panky goin' on here, me thinks!* After snapping off some photos of the pair when they left the hotel, Bob returned to his parking spot in the ABP employee lot.

A black Infiniti arrived and parked in one of the executive slots. *This is a new one.* Bob was able to get several still shots off before the driver's image evaporated into the glare on the back window of Bob's surveillance van. He spoke notes into a recorder: *White male, over six feet, tight crew cut, athletic, confident type. Maybe ex-military?*

"Julie, tell me what it was like to work at ABP." Mack spoke softly, knowing that her physical pain and all she'd been through would make it difficult to think about what went on before the day Henry died. Mack leaned in to listen until their eyes met and he nodded gently. *My God, she's tough. The way she's been beat up, I'm surprised she can talk at all.*

"Oh, I don't know. Probably not much different I imagine from any other bio-pharm company. There were deadlines to meet and procedural disagreements mostly, like in any lab.

"Tell me more about the people. You mentioned Wendy Hewitt?"

"Yeah, she was our boss. Her boss was Dr. McGinn. She was tough, a real pain in the butt. She was always pressuring Henry, but he thought it was coming from McGinn. We knew there was more to those two."

"How so? And by 'we' you mean you and Henry?"

"Yeah. Henry interrupted them making out in a storage room. He said they turned and saw him before he could back away. Embarrassing, ya know? "

"Hmm. What else?"

"Wendy insisted that Henry continue testing on the rats until he could come up with notes that met the requirements of the protocol, but she meant for him to make it happen the way they wanted, regardless of what Henry found."

"That doesn't sound normal."

"Absolutely not." Becoming more animated, she explained, "Henry saw rats reacting badly to the testing. But Hewitt didn't care. She kept after Henry continuously. He was really worried about the protocol being moved along too quickly and someone ending up hurt."

Julie's face clouded after mentioning Henry and her voice trailed off. She put her head down a moment then looked up at Mack and her mouth tightened.

"Look, I've been working in lab settings long enough to know you don't let the desired outcome dictate the means of getting there. Hey, anyone can disagree on the approach to a project; but fudging the methodology and data to arrive at preferred conclusions? That's not science, it's fraud. Falsifying lab results is very serious and Henry didn't want any part of it."

Mack thought a second or two, then asked, "But doesn't the FDA have strict parameters and rules to follow before a drug reaches the public? I heard it takes years."

"That's true, but one of the early phases, and the most important ones, involves testing on humans. Initially, it is a small control group, but it's still human testing. The thought of humans being subjected to risk because of false data worried Henry a lot."

"Yeah, I guess it would."

Chapter *Thirteen*

Maria and Sofia boarded a bus after Sofia's eighth drug trial session, and 10 minutes into the ride Sofia began screaming at the top of her lungs.

"You're all trying to kill me. No one understands."

"No one is after you, Mama. It's Maria. I'm here." But Sofia's agitation was beyond verbal persuasion. Both her hands tightly grasped the bar at the top of the seat ahead of her. Her eyes wide, her head flailing around in hysterics, Sofia was in another world—a world beyond communication, beyond reason.

"Mama, let go. It's okay. It's okay." But Sofia kept wailing at the top of her lungs. The bus came to a stop and the driver walked down the aisle.

Sofia shrieked, "Here he comes. Diablo! You cannot have me!" She released her grip, slid into the aisle and —with surprising agility—ran at the bus driver with clawed-hands raised. The bus driver drew back defensively, as Sofia tried to rake his face.

It took both Maria and the bus driver to restrain Sofia until she went limp, still babbling incoherently. One of the other riders called 911, so when the two-man patrol car arrived, they gently took Sofia off the bus and back to Somerset Hospital.

Once her mother was sedated, breathing normally and somewhat lucid again, Maria left her in the ER and went upstairs to where the drug trial was being conducted. She confronted the program administrator.

"What is going on here? My mother totally freaked out a few minutes after drug infusion. She has never been a violent person. She was hallucinating and attacked a bus driver. It can only be your test drug behind this." She moved closer to the administrator and added, "And I want answers now!"

The administrator tried to calm Maria. He admitted that in drug trials there can be unexpected reactions and side effects. "Each patient has a different tolerance level. I will check her chart and we will adjust her amounts downward. We'll monitor her more closely, Maria. When you come from now on, you and Sofia should hang around for an hour or so before leaving. That way we can keep closer tabs on her reaction."

His tone was conciliatory and what he said made sense to Maria. He went on. "In fact, let's do an EEG each time before you leave. Measuring her brain waves will give us an idea of how her neurons are reacting to the drug."

The administrator added, "I hope you understand. To some extent, we are in new territory here, Maria. Much about dementia is still unknown and these drug trials are teaching moments for us all. As a medical person, yourself, I'm sure you understand there are many variables involved. That's what a drug trial is—testing. We are carefully following the protocol. Please be patient."

Mack decided to interview Wendy Hewitt away from the security of her workplace, so he waited outside her townhouse in Raritan. Bob had provided times and vehicle descriptions in his reports, so Mack knew what she would be driving and when to expect her homecoming.

When Wendy Hewitt parked her Honda and got out, Mack approached. He knew spontaneous interviewing is very revealing but has to be done carefully, especially with anyone who might feel threatened. He stood off at a respectful distance, his head slanted in an inquiring way, and called out, "Ms. Hewitt?" He smiled.

Wendy spun around, surprised. She braced, not sure of what to expect. "Who are you? She blinked a couple times and challenged Mack. "And why were you waiting for me in front of my home?"

Mack held his investigator identification out in front and very slowly continued his approach. "I am a licensed New Jersey private investigator, Ms. Hewitt. I'm here conducting an investigation of a fatal accident. You know, the one where Henry Lott was killed?"

Still maintaining a defensive posture, Wendy slowly nodded her head. "Oh, that was terrible." Then she frowned. "I don't see how I could help you with that."

"Well, you see, I am trying to look at every angle. I know you were his supervisor, and it seems Mr. Lott was having some problems at work. Putting that together with no solid cause for the accident—" Mack paused. "Anyway, there are unanswered questions. See what I mean?"

Looking away and fingering her keys, Wendy started moving up the walk toward her front door. "No, I don't see what you mean. What are you trying to say?"

Mack trailed behind, keeping pace with Wendy. "Well, it's just that I always cover all the bases and it looks like there could be something more to this so-called "accident."

Mack let that sink in, then said, "Henry's family is entitled to know what happened and my job is to find it out, Ms. Hewitt. That's why I'm here." Mack stared at her, waiting for a response.

"I see. What can I say?" Avoiding eye contact, she followed up with a rapid-fire response that didn't surprise Mack. "He was a good employee. He never gave me any problems. He worked hard and was good at it. We are all saddened by his death. Would you tell the family that for me, please? Now I have to get inside. I have some errands to run. You'll have to excuse me." With that, she turned and hurriedly withdrew into the safety of her condo.

Mack yelled after her, "Thank you, Ms. Hewitt. I have more questions . . . Ms. Hewitt?" Mack's experience told him Wendy's nervously delivered volley of short sentences was defensive. That—taken together with her retreat from further questioning—was telling. Mack thought, *Typical avoidance reaction. She's hiding something.*

Mack switched off his pocket recorder and spoke into his cell phone. "Bob, she's primed. She's all yours."

"Roger chief. You kill 'em, I cook 'em." Bob was set up on the next block where he could watch for any visitors or follow her if she left.

Ten minutes later Wendy came out of her condo, and Bob picked up her Honda as it passed in front of him. From Raritan, Wendy drove South on Route 206. Bob laughed and, in a sing-song voice said, "I know where you're going." He passed her, dropped his van in Princeton Country Lodge's parking lot, and quickly took a seat in front of the check-in counter and coffee kiosk. He took out his cell phone and put his thumbs to work mimicking an engrossing texting session. When Wendy arrived a minute later, Bob was just any hotel guest.

Wendy looked around the room expectantly. She took a seat opposite Bob and tapped her foot nervously. Bob kept pecking away at his phone, smiling and nodding his head, now and then. He paid her no mind.

When Dr. Peter McGinn showed up, Wendy got up and started in on him. "Why the hell is a private. . ."

McGinn shushed her. "Why don't you get a megaphone?" He looked around uncomfortably and took her by the arm, guiding her to a table a couple of steps away. Bob couldn't hear every word, but he heard enough.

"What have you done, Peter? Why would a private detective be waiting for me in my front yard?" Her face flushed, Wendy was demanding answers.

In a firm, yet soothing voice, McGinn said, "We've done nothing. There's nothing to worry about." He leaned in closer. "Listen to me. It's probably just some crackpot P.I. poking around. I wouldn't give it another thought."

Wendy adamantly shook her head. "He didn't act like a crackpot. He was confrontative and serious. He knew just what he was doing, Peter. I'm frightened." Then, as if catching on, she asked, "Wait a minute. What did you mean when you said, 'We've done nothing?' Are you talking about you and that Archer guy that's been hanging around? I don't like him one bit."

With that, an elderly housekeeper started up a vacuum cleaner at the other end of the lobby. The noise was just loud enough to prevent Bob from overhearing his targets. But when Bob glanced up, he saw that their conversation had escalated into a full-blown argument. Sitting back, McGinn was adamantly shaking his head as Wendy, leaning forward in her chair, was assertively pressing him. She was not taking his "no" for an answer.

From his van, Bob called Mack. "Looks like we got some action, boss. I just overheard a conversation you won't believe or maybe you will." He gave it over to Mack, word-for-word, along with characterizing the couple's argument at the end.

Mack thought out loud, "Why would she ask McGinn, 'What have you done?' And the name, 'Archer.' Does that ring any bells?" Mack jotted notes of their conversation.

Bob said, "Nah. Could be he's the guy in the Infiniti, though. That guy looked out of place at ABP."

"Bob, why don't you stop in at the office and speed up Nezzie on researching that guy. Have her start with a plate lookup on his car."

Chapter *Fourteen*

Maria **parked on the top level** of the Bridgewater Commons parking garage. She and Sofia had just left the drug trial and agreed that a little shopping might be an enjoyable break from the non-stop tension that had recently filled their lives.

"Come, Mama. We can eat in Salad Works and take a walk around the mall." They had a pleasant lunch and Sofia conversed surprisingly well. "You're having a good day, Mama. I can tell."

Sofia smiled back and commented on a young couple nearby. "You can't tell the boys from the girls anymore, Maria."

Maria said, "I think this new drug will help you remember things better. What do you think?"

"I think so. I was so confused before, but now I think I see things better in my head," Sofia answered hopefully.

Maria hung close to Sofia as they shopped, watching for any adverse reaction to the hustle and bustle of the crowded mall. They looked like any other mother-daughter pair sharing a pleasant outing together. Arm in arm, they walked. They carried their packages up the escalator to the upper level of the garage where Maria's car was parked. Then everything changed.

A man in a dark suit at the other end of the row of cars approached on his way into the mall. The sun was at his back, so he appeared as a dark shadow the nearer he came. Sofia slowed and clutched Maria's arm. "It's Diablo again! Run, Maria, he's after us."

"No, Mama. It's just a man going into the mall." Maria turned to Sofia to hold her close, but Sofia pulled away and, screaming gibberish, ran off to the right with Maria in pursuit. Maria caught up with her and grabbed at Sofia's coat. As they neared the waist-high parapet on the roof, Sofia ripped away from Maria's grip and flung herself over the edge into space.

"Mama, NO!"

Sofia's screeching abruptly ended two seconds later with a hideous thump.

"Come in, Dr. McGinn." Mark Lott held the door open and led the executive into the living room of the modest Lott home. The French doors to the dining room were closed with the curtains drawn, isolating Melanie Lott from the conversation to come.

Mark explained, "Since Henry's passing, mother has been in no condition to receive visitors."

McGinn, the fastidious executive, sat forward on the edge of a worn, stuffed chair across from Mark and Julie. Although clean and tidy, the living room was decorated with decades-old furniture, its walls displaying family photographs and inexpensive artwork. The sofa wore a throw that failed in its duty to completely hide threadbare spots along its armrests. The rug was frayed at its edges and one lampshade hung slightly askance, its clip-on fitter bent out of shape. The Lott home reminded McGinn of his own humble beginnings in Pennsylvania's coal country. By cheating and conniving, he had clawed his way up the corporate ladder, vowing never to live near the poverty-line again. Now—perched uncomfortably in a setting similar to his childhood—those thoughts flashed through his mind before coming back to the point of his visit. *Okay, Alfred, time to get on with your bullshit victim visit.*

"I want you both to know that the company is so very sorry for your loss. And, Julie, it is good to see you up and around. I kept track of your progress in the hospital. You're a brave girl."

Julie was working hard to restrain herself. She and Mark agreed to let McGinn do the talking but she couldn't let him get away with the "brave girl" comment. "Dr. McGinn, there's nothing brave about it. I had no choice—and I'm not a girl anymore."

"Of course. That was a bad choice of words. Frankly, I find discussing this with you a bit awkward, because I should've been here a long time ago."

Mark quietly cast a mildly sarcastic glance at McGinn. He wanted to strike the right tone: not hostile but not overly obliging, either. He answered, "Mother hasn't been the same since Henry . . ." Using the word '*died*' was still difficult. "He lived here with her, you know." He looked intently at McGinn. "I know he always gave his best to ABP and I hoped the company would step up and show some sympathy. So, I'm glad you finally came. I will let my mother know." He offered a half-hearted smile.

McGinn continued, "Well, I just want to say that Henry was a good and loyal employee and we miss his steady and balanced presence in the laboratory. His supervisor, Wendy Hewitt, has not been able to find a satisfactory replacement yet."

Julie reflected, "Yes, he was loyal. He was also good at what he did. I miss him, too."

McGinn found conversation less thorny once he started going over the death benefit to which Henry's mother was entitled. He read some of the fine print aloud and finished up with, "Here is the claim release, Mark. If you could have your mother sign and return it to our HR department, I will see that they issue a check quickly."

A self-conscious moment of silence followed. McGinn cleared his throat, and stood up, happy to be free of the lumpy old chair. He said, "I must go now but be assured, Julie, your job is waiting for you when you're ready to return."

Mark stood and walked McGinn to the door. "Just one more thing, Dr. McGinn. In Henry's diary he noted how much he loved working at ABP and with his friends in the lab. Any chance you could follow this visit up with a personal letter to my mother? It would mean a lot to her." He turned to Julie. "He mentioned you a lot in that diary, too."

Unable to conceal his alarm, McGinn's voice quavered. "He had a diary?"

"Oh, yes." Mark did his best to keep a straight face. "I just glanced at it and haven't read through it, but from the time he was a kid he kept a diary about his personal life and, later on, his work life. It looks like a lot of scientific gobbledygook to me, but he was always writing in that diary." His expression almost piteous, Mark piled it on. "Henry was a very private person. He was better at writing things down than having conversations."

Julie joined them at the doorway. "I didn't know he kept a diary. What did he say about me?"

"I only started to read it, Julie, but it's really clear he really liked you. Reading between the lines, anyone could tell he was in love with you. We should read it together sometime." Mark took a deep breath. "Before I gave the diary to mother, I noticed the last entry was dated the day he died. Our mother holds the diary close." Mark turned back to McGinn and said, "It's all she has left of him."

McGinn hurriedly shook Mark's hand and said, "I appreciate your understanding. I will personally see to the letter. Bye, now." Sliding into his Volvo, he thought anxiously, *A fuckin' diary? Christ! Better call Archer.*

Mark ushered Julie through the French doors and to the edge of Melanie Lott's bed. The aging matriarch smiled playfully and asked, "Did he go for it?"

Mark chuckled, "Oh yeah, Mother. He bit like a rat on cheese. You should've seen his face."

Julie was confused. "What about the diary?"

"There is no diary, Julie," Melanie smirked, "but he doesn't know that." She pulled Mark closer. "You did record it, right?"

"Yup. I'll play if for you."

Chapter *Fifteen*

iego's saddened face, deep lines across his forehead and
darkness under his eyes, pressed closer to the visitor glass.

"How did it happen?"

"One minute she was fine, having a good time, and the
next she was someone else, Uncle." Maria's face revealed her
anguish. "She pulled away from me and jumped off the top
of the building. I tried, Uncle." Her voice trailed off, her head
shaking in disbelief, her lips trembling.

Controlling his rising anger, and in as soft a voice as he
could muster, he whispered into the intercom, "It was that
drug test, wasn't it, child?"

Maria could only nod her head. She finally blurted, "It's
my fault. I was so sure it was working."

Diego's face darkened. He intertwined his fingers and
squeezed hard against his chest. His hands whitened from
the pressure. A moment later, his emotional control regained,

Diego's expression softened and he said, "No, it's not your fault, Maria. It's not your fault."

At that moment Diego's face was that of the compassionate uncle, but then it changed to the malevolent drug-dealing criminal. His jaw clenched tight, the real Diego Gomez materialized, his countenance a slit-eyed vicious portrait of hate. "Go home, Maria, and bury my sister, your mama. I will handle this from now on." *Muerte por muerte!*

"You did what?" Attorney Reddy and Mack almost said it in shocked unison.

Mark repeated. "We let McGinn, that vice-president at ABP, think Henry kept a diary. We baited the trap and we are waiting for him to make the next move." Mark played the recording for the group, sitting smugly in a side chair, his fingertips tented in an aloof pose, pleased with himself.

"I don't believe this." Mack's dander was up. "Don't you understand we are dealing with very dangerous people here? Ever think they might go to any length to destroy that diary or take you out like they did Henry? He turned to attorney

Reddy, shaking his head in disgust, waiting for Reddy to say something.

"Mack's right, Mark. Not only did you step out of line by acting on your own, you've likely put yourselves in danger."

Bob Higgins strolled along the far wall, fingering the lawyer's bookshelves, quiet until now. In a subdued voice—the kind that gets attention—he threw out an idea. "Yeah. Not good. But maybe there's a way to divert their interest from Mark and his mother. Maybe we can capitalize on this screwup somehow."

The "Mack and Bob team" locked eyes. Mack spoke first. "Okay, maybe there is a way." Speaking slowly and making it up as he went along, he picked up on Bob's thought. "So, I go to ABP and talk to McGinn about my conversation with Wendy Hewitt, and—" He paused and looked to Bob to make sure he was with him.

Bob hesitated, then said, "and in that conversation, you let it slip that you have the diary. That way, it's off Mark and his mother, Melanie, and on us, and—"

Mack wrapped it up. "and we can set up a sting while keeping them off Maria, too."

Avery Reddy's head was bouncing back and forth during the exchange. He said, "Are you guys nuts? If this is what we think it is, you guys are putting yourselves in real danger."

"Right, Avery." Mack winked at Bob. "That's what we do. This ain't one of your cultured legal depositions, my friend. This is not checkers. It's real-world chess, and the key is to be one move ahead of the other guy. If we can't do this, we don't deserve to be in this business."

Bob Higgins said, "Yeah, and now it's our turn to make a move."

Mark had something more to say. "Okay, there's no diary, but this may be really important. Julie just told me she remembered my brother telling her he kept and hid his original notes—the ones that show the test results for what they really are." He then made a sour face. "Trouble is, she has no idea where he hid them."

Attorney Reddy couldn't resist the irony. He said, "I don't believe this: They will be looking for a diary that doesn't exist and we will be looking for notes that do, and they don't know about the notes, but we do, yet we have no clue where they are. How crazy is this?"

Mack answered, "Crazy, but crazy good, if we can find those notes. We need them. They could make the whole case, including a motive."

Avery grinned.

On the way out, Bob told Mack a joke, but it was really directed at their attorney pal.

"Mack, what does a lawyer get when you give him Viagra?"

Reddy yelled, "No more goddamn lawyer jokes!"

Mack's raised eyebrows signaled Bob to finish the joke.

Ignoring Avery's protest, Bob delivered the punchline. "The lawyer gets taller, of course."

Chapter *Sixteen*

Archer was beginning to regret taking on this job. "A
diary? You mean that little jerk wrote stuff down that
could come back and bite us in the ass? And why did you visit
them in the first place?"

"A diary. That's what Lott's brother said." McGinn was
wringing his hands. He explained, "My boss ordered me to
convey ABP's condolences and to handle the death benefit
paperwork. That's normal practice. I had to do it." McGinn's
brow was tightly knitted, his eyes darting about the office. "I
never expected a diary." He was sweating.

Exasperated, Archer said, "Don't you think if there
was anything damaging in that diary, it would've come
out by now?"

McGinn said, "Not necessarily. When I left them, I was
led to believe that no one had really gotten into it yet. But
once Julie gets her hands on that diary, it's all over. She'll
understand the technical parts. She will be a big problem."

He stopped fidgeting and stared at Archer, quizzically cocking his head.

Archer read McGinn's unspoken message. "So, do we kill everybody involved? Is that your solution? This is a lot more than I signed up for, so you'd better show me a few more zeroes." Archer didn't let it go at that. "This company stands to make a billion or more on this new drug, so you gotta pony up, pal."

"Don't worry about the money. I have another 50K in my discretionary account and I can always get more from Alfred. But what about the diary? You're the expert"

This was the first time one of their conversations became confrontational. McGinn, the normally smooth control freak, was rattled.

Still on the subject of money, Archer demanded, "Okay, but I want half now. Today."

McGinn nodded and made a note.

Archer addressed the diary issue, feeling like he was teaching fourth grade. "First, no matter what's in that diary, there's no way anyone could connect it—or us—to Henry Lott's checking out or the crash. Right? That would be a major leap without any evidence."

"I suppose so, but something else has come up." McGinn squirmed around in his executive chair uncomfortably. "We, uh . . ." He couldn't seem to get it out.

"What?!?!" Archer's head jutted forward, on the edge of losing his patience altogether.

"A private investigator tried to interview Wendy about Lott's accident." McGinn's voice rose an octave and he quickly rattled off, "But she didn't tell him anything because she doesn't know anything about . . . you know."

Archer's eyes narrowed and his lips tightened. The skin on the back of his neck tingled, triggering that old survival alarm that had served him so well in the past when danger threatened. Flickering images tore through his mind: *Zimbabwe, Colombia, Yemen.*

He spoke resolutely. Menacingly. Icily. "I see. And what was said in that interview?"

McGinn went over what Wendy Hewitt related to him at the Princeton Country Lodge, with no omissions. Then he tried to say, "But I don't think . . ."

A raised palm stopped him. The professional soldier of fortune was in command of the moment. He approached the problem like any of the deadly exercises in his past. Methodically. Logically. He analyzed aloud, "The guy's fishing. He uses a cold approach—no appointment—to throw her off guard. He hints he knows something about Henry Lott's death and that it had something to do with the company, inferring the company could be implicated somehow. But he doesn't know. He's guessing." But Archer knew it was problematic, because the guy was professional. *A P.I. who knows the drill. That sucks! Someone has come up with a theory of Henry's death being connected to his troubles in the lab, and that doesn't come out of thin air.*

"Do you think he will be a problem?" McGinn was out of his depth and he knew it.

"We'll see. Let me worry about that. As to the diary, even if Henry's technical notes go against what you're trying to do, you can always begin a campaign to discredit the little jerk."

"You don't understand." McGinn whined on, "Wendy's been pushing him into falsifying paperwork in the protocol. Presumably, the diary contains the actual results of his research. And that would put us in deep shit." Their exchange was suddenly interrupted.

Flouting decorum, CEO Alfred Stewart entered McGinn's office unannounced, his face ashen. He blubbered, "Peter, I just learned a woman in the initial drug trial committed suicide. This is terrible." Regaining composure, he said, "Oh, I'm sorry, I didn't know you had a guest."

"That's okay, Alfred. This is Ted Archer, our new security consultant. Ted, meet our president and CEO, Alfred Stewart."

They shook hands. "Pleased to meet you, Ted, and welcome aboard. Peter has told me good things about you."

Archer nodded, but cast a querulous look at McGinn, receiving back a barely perceptible negative head shake. Archer was relieved. *Okay, you didn't bring the boss in on the Henry Lott job. Good thing!*

Alfred continued, anxiety etched on his face. "Peter, this has never happened before. A suicide." He collapsed into a side chair, thoroughly dispirited. "Other than putting the trial on hold for now, how do you suggest we handle this new development?"

McGinn glanced over at Archer and lamented, "Suicide in a drug trial. Not good."

Head up and neck stiffened in his best confident corporate stance, McGinn continued, "I'll take care of it Alfred. I'll pull back the trial for now and take a closer look at that suicide." *Shit! Everything's unraveling.*

Archer looked unfazed as his mind churned on the news. He'd survived a lot of close calls because his first instinct was to view an obstacle as a potential advantage. *All it usually takes is a little finessing.*

A gifted schemer, he thought, *A suicide in the drug trial, huh? If Lott falsified or didn't falsify his lab notes, what does it matter? He could still be accused of it. Hey, maybe suicide could explain his accident, too.* Biting his lower lip, Archer's thoughts landed on the obvious. *We need to get our hands on that diary.*

Despite a myriad of conflicting notions, and still outwardly composed, Archer managed a brief but confident smile toward McGinn. He turned to ABP's third-generation bio-mogul and commented, "I might have a few ideas on handling things, Mr. Stewart."

"Then I leave it to you two, Peter." And with that, Alfred Stewart headed for the door, his head down and shoulders sagging. "Suicide. I can't believe it."

After a few moments weighing all options, Archer said, "If that diary shows up, you're screwed. It's not just the end of your career. This could all unravel and you'll be in the joint a long, long time."

McGinn said, "You know, you're in this too, so we better do *something*."

Archer laughed. "Me? Hell, I'll be long gone before they even come for you. You forget, McGinn, I'm a survivor." After an uncomfortable moment of silence passed between them, Archer muttered, "Yeah, that fuckin' diary. Gotta get it."

McGinn sighed quietly. His gaze through the office window landed on 20-some Canadian geese sheltering in reeds at the north end of the retention pond. It reminded him of when, as a youngster, he looked up in awe at V-formed geese gliding south in the late fall high over Carbondale, Pennsylvania. *Life was hard, but simpler then. This life is so complicated, more complicated every day.*

Chapter *Seventeen*

When Julie heard about Sofia's suicide, she immediately called Mark Lott.

"Mark, one of my co-workers at ABP just told me a woman in the drug trial just killed herself. I told you Henry was right about those agitated and unstable lab rats. If only we had his 14168-ALZ notes."

"I guess I shouldn't be surprised, Julie. Looks like Henry knew what he was talking about. Let's get together with the lawyer again and see what he makes of this."

Reddy, Mack, and Bob sat across from Mark and Julie in the small conference room of Reddy's Westfield office. Julie repeated what she'd heard about Sofia's suicide and that human testing had been temporarily suspended pending further review, according to the administrator of the drug trial.

"Evenson, that physician's assistant, put it this way, 'Due to several atypical incidents, the investigational trial is on hold for now.'" Julie shook her head in disgust. "Do you believe that? 'Atypical incidents.' So corporate and unfeeling!"

Mark slid forward in his chair, "See? My brother knew. He knew the drug was not ready for testing on humans. And now, not only did someone commit suicide, others in the trial may have suffered adverse effects, as well."

Mack elbowed Bob, as he rose. "We'll get right on it. Once we identify the suicide victim, we'll talk to the family and see what they know." Heading toward the door, Mack threw over his shoulder, "And don't you two go off and pull any stunts like you did with McGinn and the so-called diary."

Once in the parking lot, Mack said, "Bob, I'll get Nezzie going on identifying the suicide and the follow-up with that. Why don't you talk to this Evenson guy? It might help us figure out what direction to go in next."

Inez Winston was Mack's trusted and more-than-secretary assistant. Her tweezed, arched eyebrows and heavy makeup gave her a tough looking exterior, but "Nezzie," as Mack affectionately called her, was anything but. At 62 and a widow, she had a soft spot for Mack and Bob. She referred to them as, "My boys," and was not above kidding around with them now and then. She managed the office and did whatever she could to provide office research while Mack and Bob were in the field. "I'll get right on it, boss. There should at least be a news article or two on a suicide."

Mack parked in one of ABP's visitor spots and pushed through the heavy glass door. He gave the receptionist his business card and said, "I am here to speak with Dr. McGinn. I don't have an appointment, but I'm sure he'll see me." Mack didn't wait for a response. He nonchalantly turned around, eased onto a guest sofa and opened a magazine.

Mack was right. McGinn's secretary took only a couple of minutes to arrive and guide Mack to McGinn's corner office.

"What can we do for you, uh, Mr. Mackey?" McGinn fingered Mack's card nervously, but otherwise, seemed self-assured.

"Nice office." Mack sauntered around McGinn's suite and paused to peer through the window at the geese calmly floating on the pond without a care in the world. He said nothing for a long moment. He just looked around the office.

"Ahem, again, Mr. Mackey, why are you here?" He had a trace of a smile, his demeanor seemingly unruffled.

"Mr. McGinn, I spoke to—or tried to speak to—your Wendy Hewitt about Henry Lott. I'm sure you remember him."

McGinn stiffened, "It's *Doctor* McGinn, and what about Henry? We lost a good employee in such a tragic accident. Miss Hewitt, his supervisor, reported your attempt to talk to her. You startled her. She also thought you were suggesting something other than a simple auto accident was involved." McGinn took up his position of authority behind his desk, motioning Mack into a side chair. "Just what is on your mind, sir?"

"Henry's brother, Mark, has the idea that Henry was having problems at work and hired me to look into it. I'm not sure where this is going, uh, *Doctor* McGinn, but I thought I would go to the top to try and find out. Was he having problems?"

"Surely, Mr. Mackey, you must see this as an odd request. Even if there were a problem, I would not be at liberty to discuss that with you, would I?"

"I'll take that as a 'Yes.'" Mack thought, *Now, do it now.* "You know, of course, Dr. McGinn, Henry kept a diary. Mark turned it over to me for examination. We are hiring a forensic psychologist to review it and evaluate Henry's mental stability in the days leading up to the accident. The police theorize it

100

was a suicide, lacking any other logical explanation. But the family simply cannot accept that. I am trying to give them closure." Mack feigned indignation. "I hate that word: *closure*. What does it mean, anyway? He's gone."

"Oh, I see. You want to check with us to determine whether or not we made any observations of Henry that would help clear the suicide theory up, one way or the other."

"Something like that," Mack replied with a raised-eyebrow that said, "So?"

McGinn replied, "I'd like to help you out here, Mr. Mackey, but my hands are tied right now. Let me check with our attorney to see what we can legally share about Mr. Lott and I'll get back to you. Maybe there is a way."

They shook hands. A few minutes later Mack started his Range Rover and snickered out loud, "Hook, line and sinker!"

Chapter *Eighteen*

McGinn, slightly relieved by the tone of Mack's visit, sent a text to Archer. "Call me. Things look better. More on diary, but good!"

Archer read the text and was furious. He called McGinn back. "Before you say anything, McGinn, understand this: We will *not* be specific during phone calls or texts. No texts. No voice messages. Not even a goddamn smoke signal. Got it?"

"Okay, okay. Don't get so upset. Just come in and we'll talk."

Archer was early for his appointment with McGinn. He stopped short of his ABP employee parking space and slipped into the larger lot to blend in with other vehicles. Reaching under his seat, he retrieved a small audio receiver and powered it up from the cigarette lighter outlet in the Infiniti. Just as he had prior to every meeting with McGinn when in range, he patiently sat and took in whatever was going on in McGinn's office. Most of the time he overheard mundane chatter associated with whatever was on McGinn's work schedule that day. Today, however, was different. Much different.

"Peter, I haven't been able to sleep, I will not be pushed to the side and told, 'Don't worry about it.'" Wendy Hewitt's voice came across bordering on hysteria. "What have you and Archer done? Please tell me you had nothing to do with Henry Lott's death. Peter, tell me it was an accident."

Archer held the receiver closer, moving the small antenna around to improve reception. His heartbeat quickened.

"Stop it, Wendy! Someone will hear you." Archer heard a door slam.

"I don't care. Talk to me, Peter. Why was that investigator talking to me the other day and not you?"

"He did talk to me, Wendy. All he wants is to find out if it was a suicide or not. There's nothing more to it." McGinn sounded conciliatory. "Now go back to work. No more of this."

"What is going on here? You are not telling me everything and it scares me. I will not be a party to anything illegal. It was enough that I pushed and pushed Henry to alter his notes on 14168-ALZ. Now someone has died in the drug trial and maybe because I followed your orders."

Archer could hear Wendy quietly sobbing. A short pause. The door slammed again. McGinn could be heard sighing.

103

Archer frowned and turned off the monitor while moving to his own parking space. *This bitch is gonna be a problem.*

McGinn met Archer at his office door. "Good news! The diary is now in the hands of that private eye I was talking about."

"How can that be good?" *What a doofus!*

"Well, it's good because Julie doesn't have access to it now; but that's not the only reason I wanted to talk to you." McGinn was trying to reassure himself. "We now know the reason for the P.I. trying to talk to Wendy. It seems Lott's family doesn't like the suicide label on Henry and they hired him to check into it. He hasn't a clue to Lott's death, other than the suicide theory."

Archer pressed McGinn into relating the entire discussion between him and the P.I. The cold, calculating security expert took it all in and, after a moment's consideration, said, "What I see here is a smart play by that guy. Strategically, he had nothing to lose by visiting you and everything to gain by trying to throw you off." Archer's disgusted expression emphasized his words, "For all your education, you are such a simpleton, Peter."

McGinn, now off balance, whimpered, "I don't think so. He seemed so sincere. I just can't believe . . ."

His face inches away from McGinn's, Archer poked his index finger hard into the executive's pudgy mid-section and sneered, "You need to stop being a dick head, Peter. Everything's changed. You are in *my world* now. We're in this together and our survival depends on my hard-learned skills, not your sniveling and naïve impressions."

Archer began to pace. "You've been had, pal. That P.I. was on an exploratory mission. He did two things. He set you at ease about Lott's accident by mentioning suicide. And he intentionally wanted you to believe he had the diary, so we'd give up on looking for it." Then, out of the blue, Archer inquired, "By the way, what is your relationship with Wendy?"

McGinn's face reddened. "That is *none* of your business, Ted."

Archer entered McGinn's space again. "It is as long as my ass is on the line, right next to yours, you idiot!"

Puffing up, McGinn came back with, "You can't talk to me that . . ."

Archer waved McGinn's words away. "I will talk to you any way I want. And you will listen. That is, if you want to stay out of jail—or worse!" Archer glared right through McGinn.

Archer had another demand. "You will also get me the rest of that fifty grand now." With a sour face, he said, "It looks like I'll be around a while cleaning up this mess."

Peter McGinn, until now the always-confident, in-charge and pompous executive, folded like a deck chair on the *Titanic*. "Whatever you say," he said softly. "You're right, of course. I'm out of my element, here." After a short pause, he asked, "What do we do now?"

"*We* do nothing. I will handle everything from here on in. You will report to me every day. I want to know who contacts you, what they say and do, and all you can pick up about them—everything." Archer rooted around in his briefcase and handed McGinn a throw-away phone. "You will call me on this, and only on this, understand?"

McGinn nodded. Eyes lowered and shoulders slumped, his voice almost a whisper, he answered Archer's earlier question. "Wendy and I are lovers."

Archer couldn't suppress a mocking grin. He thought, *I knew this guy was a cupcake in the beginning.* "Try not to fuck your part up, okay?" Archer left a stunned and shaken McGinn in his wake. The meeting was over, giving rise to a new protocol at Analytic Bio-Pharma. A protocol controlled by Theodore "Ted" Archer.

"Mack, I got some goodies for ya. Some good and some a little short on particulars." Nezzie, forever the diligent researcher, was reporting in after all morning and half the afternoon bent over the office computer.

"Shoot, kiddo."

"I found an obit on the suicide lady. She took a nose-dive off the roof of the Bridgewater Mall. She was Sofia Rodriguez, 64, had two kids, Jose and Maria, both adults at home. I'll text you the last address for her."

"Great. Anything on that name, 'Archer,' that Bob overheard at the hotel?"

"Nada. Dead end. I don't even know if that's a first or last name, Mack. I did run that plate Bob picked up at ABP and it comes up on a new Infiniti Q-70 registered to an Ecuadorian company, *La Cruz -Agro Compania*. I searched the company in that new source we found, *Open Source Corporations, Worldwide*. Nada. Nothing. The company doesn't seem to exist."

"Hmm. How do you get a car registered in New Jersey to a phony international corporation? *I wonder if Archer is the guy Bob spotted in that Infiniti at ABP? Probably.*

"Thanks, Nezzie. Keep punchin' on Archer and that foreign company. They might go together."

"Oh, one more thing." He caught Nezzie before she disconnected. "Do you have the Owens girl's phone number? I want to take her with me when I visit the Rodriguez family."

"You got it, boss. I'll include that in the text."

"My angel!"

Chapter *Nineteen*

etrieval of the private investigator's business card from McGinn was all Archer needed to flesh out the rest of Mack's identification and locate his office. He waited and tailed Mack to the Rodriguez garden apartment in South Plainfield.

As Mack and Julie approached the Rodriguez apartment door, Julie said, "Mack, I'm not an investigator. I don't think I would know what to say. You should do the talking."

"Actually, Julie, I want you to say whatever's on your mind. That's the reason I asked you to come along. We may need their help and, in this instance, someone other than an investigator could bring them around better to our thinking."

Jose's greeting was frosty. He led them into the living room where his older sister was seated. Her hostility obvious, Maria confronted Julie. "You are the one who works for the company that made the drug that killed our mama, right?"

Mack reacted first, putting his hands up. "Now, hold on . . ."

"It's okay, Mack." Julie stopped him. "Yes, I did work for Analytic Bio-Pharm until they tried to kill me."

Maria's eyebrows squinched together as she said, "What do you mean?"

Julie took a breath and, with Mack chiming in, described the accident and her injuries and how Henry was killed.

Pausing for a moment, Mack went on about how suspicious the rapid acceleration was. Julie then explained the role she and Henry had in the drug protocol and how Henry agonized over the pressure he was under to falsify data. By the time they finished, the chilly reception had completely thawed.

Maria cried, "Oh my God. Then it looks like we are on the same side, no?" Jose's softened look said he agreed.

Maria went on to explain her mother's initial dementia diagnosis and how she came to be in the drug trial, along with all the ups and downs that went with it. She choked up several times. Mack and Julie nodded, listening in silence.

When Maria finished, Julie, in a very quiet and somber voice said, "There's no question in my mind. That 14168-ALZ drug trial got way ahead of itself. Henry's notes were unacceptable to the company because his truths slowed them down." Julie's eyes watered. She said, "Henry was a good man. No matter what anyone says, we know he died trying to protect people like your mother."

Mack declared, "Here's what I think. We all need to have a sit-down and go over what we know and how we can help each other out." Looking to Jose and Maria, he went on. "On our side, we have been meeting with attorney Avery Reddy in Westfield to keep this all legal and organized. Just so you know, there are things we can do, remedies in law, both civil and criminal. But we have work to do. We know you just buried your mother and are still grieving. Are you up for going in with us to go after them?"

"Yes, we are." Jose spoke first, glancing at Maria for approval. To Maria he said, "I will talk to Uncle Diego about this and. . ."

At the mention of their uncle, Maria groaned, "Do we have to bring him in?"

Perplexed, Mack asked, "Uncle Diego?"

"He is our mama's brother. They were close." Jose shot a "be quiet" look at Maria and continued. "He is Diego Gomez and he is in East Jersey State Prison in Rahway for dealing drugs—big-time drugs."

"Well, now you might as well tell them all of it." Maria's annoyance was obvious.

Jose continued. "Okay. The last time I saw him he was really pissed at the drug company and said something like, 'Don't worry. I'll handle them.'" Jose shrugged and rationalized, "Hey, Uncle Diego and mama were close. She kinda raised him."

Mack responded, "I'll talk to him. We don't need his kind of help." He thought, *that's all we need: a shootout at the ABP corral.*

Archer had no idea how long the P.I and the woman would be inside the apartment, so he wasted no time. As soon as they were out of sight, he grabbed a small metal case and crept over to the Range Rover. He dropped to all fours and then onto his back to wriggle underneath. Even though the British-made all-terrain vehicle had a sealed underbelly, it took him only 30 seconds to install the bug and the GPS unit. He'd run across these tough ones before. *Now we'll see just how much you know and how much you think you know, Mr. P.I.*

Diminished lighting didn't interfere with Archer's view, either, as he watched the two return to their Range Rover. His low-light video camera made out the facial features of the private eye and the woman, as they returned to Mack's Range Rover. Twenty-five yards away, Archer heard two distinct door-slams through his headphones and grinned.

"Mack, they seem like nice kids. Maria is so torn up." *The woman speaking.*

The engine turned over. "Yeah. I guess she feels responsible for signing her mom up for the trial." *Deeper voice, the P.I.*

"What now, Mack?"

"We set up a meeting with Avery and go from there."

Archer let them go without continuing his surveillance. His check of the GPS receiver told him he could keep track of the Range Rover from anywhere. *Now I'll scope out Henry's mother's house. Your little game didn't work on me, Mr. P.I. I want that diary, and I know just where to find it.*

Chapter *Twenty*

Sorry, Mack, wish I had better news." Avery was on speaker phone. "My accident reconstruction expert spent two full days taking apart the Lott Prius but couldn't find a damn thing that would explain the total loss of control. He says that it definitely was nothing mechanical."

"Okay, Avery. I guess we'll have to come up with something else." Mack wasn't surprised, because the state police experts came to the same conclusion. "And by the way, I checked in with the Hunterdon County Prosecutor's Office. They're not impressed with what we've come up with so far. Hey, truth be told, it isn't much."

They said, 'Come back when you have something we can investigate. We don't make accusations against our local businesses without evidence.'"

Mack went on, "I'm glad you called, anyway. We need to set up another meeting. This time we will have the kids of the woman who killed herself after being in that drug trial. They might help our case against ABP by showing that Henry was right. Their mother's death may be evidence that the drug was not ready for a human trial. And I'm about to interview another family member . . . a really interesting one. Gotta go now.".

Mack passed through the security gate and met with the sergeant in charge of visitors.

"So, you want to see Diego Gomez?" The overweight sergeant was matter-of-fact in his demeanor but couldn't resist a personal comment. "He's a nasty one. Checking any weapons?"

Mack turned over his .380 automatic and received a receipt.

The steel door opened and Diego Gomez entered the visitor's room. He looked around the room expecting Jose or Maria to wave him over. Instead he got a heads up from a guy in a suit. His first thought was, *Gotta be a cop, a Five-O. Diego doesn't do Five-O.*

Diego strolled over to the glass partition but didn't sit down. He picked up the intercom and said, "Hey, Five-0, or whoever you are, you don't get no information from Diego Gomez." He slammed down the intercom and started to walk away.

Mack said it loud enough to be heard through the glass. "Sofia Rodriguez."

Diego stopped short and his face reddened, his eyes blazing. Back on intercom, he said, "Who the fuck are you, and why do you come in here dropping my dead sister's name?"

"Calm down, tough guy. I'm not a cop. I'm a P.I. working with Jose and Maria. I'm on your side, though that's probably a first for both of us." Mack threw Diego a tight grin.

"Go ahead. Convince me." He sat down.

"Okay. Bottom line. We think the drug trial your sister was in was not ready for prime time. Numbers were dummied up at the company just to beat their competition to the punch. A young lab worker whose approval was needed refused to sign off on it. He ended up dead in a car crash. Am I getting through, Diego?"

Diego settled into his seat and leaned closer to the glass. "I'm listening."

"I've heard that you aren't too happy with the drug company, either. Right?"

"So?"

"So, I'm here to ask you to do nothing. Don't set anything in motion. I know you can get things done from in here and I don't need to be fighting you, too. I don't need interference

116

from your friends on the street while I'm putting this case together. Got it?"

With a sour expression, Diego countered, "First, *you're* not telling me what to do." A slow sly smile materialized. "Second, I don't know what you're talking about."

"Look, you and I know we'll never be on the same side on anything. But if you want to get even with the company that caused your sister's death, you will leave it to me. We already have a lawyer involved and I'm getting somewhere, so stay away." Mack stared at Diego and waited.

Diego squinted back at Mack, taking all that in. Finally, he said, "If you keep me up on what you're doing, I'll hold off for now, Five-0, but I won't wait forever."

But then Diego blinked a few times and said, "Wait. You are telling me they pulled off a phony accident?"

"We think that's what happened to the lab tech."

Diego shook his head and chuckled, "Those assholes in suits don't have the cojones to off somebody. You're stretching, Five-0."

"You're probably right, but they hired someone." Mack thought back to his conversation with Nezzie and the company with the Spanish-sounding name. "Just on a hunch, Diego, ever hear about a company . . . hold on, let me check something." Mack pulled out his file, which included the data Nezzie dug up. "Ever hear of a company known as La Cruz-Agro Compania?"

Diego sat back and belly-laughed. "Dios mio. They're still using that fake cover?"

"Who?"

"You're talking to me in here and you can't guess? C'mon, Five-O!" Gomez turned his head sideways and gave Mack a scornful look.

Mack slowly nodded. "DEA."

"Uh-huh. Cruz-Agro was an Ecuadorian export company, but it was really a front for your DEA. They offered to mule the goods from anywhere in South America to Louisiana. When one of our street dealers bit on the sting, the agents would try to jump the elevator up to the bosses. Sometimes it worked." He nodded slowly and raised his arms, palms up and looked around. "*I'm* sittin' here, right?"

"Ouch."

"So, what else you got in that file, Five-0?"

Mack looked up and said, "Does the name 'Archer' mean anything to you?"

Diego stiffened, his countenance darkened. He stared back at Mack, all casual discussion set aside. With hatred burning in his dark eyes, he asked, "What about Ted Archer?"

"You know him?"

"Ted Archer es un mal hombre." Diego spoke so forcefully, that spittle flew against the glass. "He used to be a DEA agent, before that, a Navy SEAL. Bastardo! When things didn't work like he wanted, he just went in and killed everybody. No rules, just wipe 'em out. We heard the Feds kicked him out a few years ago."

"Looks like he's back in the game on this one." Mack explained how Bob Higgins overheard Archer's name being dropped at the hotel and the Q70 Archer drove registered to the South American company found at ABP. Then Mack showed him one of the photos Bob took.

"Yeah, that's him. If you're going to play with Archer, Five-0, you better get your *best* game on. He's vicious." Diego chided Mack, "Probably too smart for you. He has tricky electronics and knows how to use them."

Now that Archer's name came up, Diego was more agreeable to cooperate with Mack. "Archer and I go way back. I lost three good men because of him. Whatever you want, you got—from me in here or out on the street. You're my new amigo, especially if you kill him."

"Amigo, huh? Just when I was getting used to Five-0." Mack smiled sarcastically. Diego put his fist against the glass. Mack matched the jailhouse handshake. "Now, don't do anything to screw me up, Diego."

As he drove away from the Rahway prison, Mack said aloud, "It's always nice to know what you're dealing with. Better crank everybody up, Mack."

Chapter *Twenty-One*

It was a sunny Sunday. **Mack and Penny** took Bob and Brenda Higgins up on an invitation for a cookout at the Higgins' country house. As they pulled up in front, Bob was on a ladder at the side of the house, repairing a cracked gutter. Back at ground level, he joked, "This is my step ladder. I never knew my real ladder." Penny groaned.

An hour later, they were settled in. "Hey, those expensive steaks are beginning to burn, Bob. Better flip 'em." Brenda Higgins was in charge of her kitchen, as well as its extension out onto the patio. "And if you two start talking business, we're gonna starve you until you can it." Penny agreed, "Yeah, no biz buzz."

After eating, Mack, Penny and their hosts enjoyed a quiet moment, leaning back in lawn chairs, having a beer and watching puffy white clouds drift around the sky. Then a humming noise violated their serenity. All four saw a small silver drone hovering about 50 feet overhead. Mack frowned, a little concerned, but Bob grinned.

"Hi, guys." A teenage boy climbed his way through the foliage between houses and joined the group. He held a device in both hands. "Hey Bob, check out my new drone."

"Hiya Ronnie. Come on in. Sit down." Bob introduced the 16-year-old to Mack and Penny. "Ronnie lives next door. He and his brother are my go-to guys when I have a computer problem."

"My computer expert is 12." Mack smiled at the boy and asked him if he would show him how to control the drone.

"This is my new one," Ronnie explained. He turned to Bob and said, "Billie hacked into my old one and took it away from me. No matter what I tried, I couldn't get my control back. He crashed it into the chimney." Ronnie chuckled. "Scared the crap out of my mom, too."

Bob and Mack reacted as one. "Say that again, Ronnie." Bob's demeanor changed from friendly to demanding. "What about hacking?" Mack stood up and waited for Ronnie to explain. Brenda started to say something, but Bob stopped her with a hurried head shake.

Ronnie explained how his brother took control of his drone. "He did a man-in-the-middle attack on my control frequency so my drone thought I was still in control."

Mack sat down hard on the picnic bench, his voiced hardened. "Archer actually did it. He really did it. Diego Gomez was right. Archer, the electronics expert, takes control of Henry Lott's car and kills him, as sure as we are sitting here."

Bob agreed. "Yeah, that would explain the lack of mechanical evidence. But what now? How do we work with this?"

Mack said, "This is above our paygrade. I know just who we should talk to about this electronics stuff."

They met in the parking lot of King's Supermarket in Whitehouse, New Jersey. Kevin Murray, a tall, white-haired, husky man in a dark suit approached, as Bob and Mack parked. "Hey, Mack. Long time no see."

"Bob, meet Kevin Murray. Kevin and I go back more than 20 years. He's *the* expert in electronic-eavesdropping detection and works for lots of major corporations and government agencies all over the world. Whenever a technical issue comes up, Kevin's the man.

"Pleased to meet you, Bob. You been putting up with Mack a long time, too?" Kevin, though soft-spoken and gentlemanly, wasn't above razzing an old friend.

Mack ignored the ribbing and got right to the point. "Bottom line, Kevin, is it possible to take over a vehicle's electronic systems and cause it to crash?"

"Actually, it's very possible. Let's walk." The trio strolled the length of the parking lot, as Kevin explained, "It's not really that new. Last year a couple of hackers caused Jeep to recall over a million vehicles when they proved they could take control of a Jeep's digital systems over the internet. If my memory serves me, there were a couple of other articles on that subject, as well. A hacker can absolutely break in and cause unintended acceleration and disable the steering and brakes. Because today's cars have so many interdependent computers onboard, spoofing messages to the car's steering or brakes is possible. Do you want to tell me more about your case?"

Mack detailed all that happened from the Lott collision to Sofia's suicide to the Diego Gomez interview. Mack ended with, "We think we know what happened, Kevin, but how do we prove the car was electronically tampered with by Archer?"

"That depends on what we can actually examine. I think you need to find some way to get to his equipment, especially his computer's memory. You have to get access to whatever he may have used to take control of Henry's car."

Disappointed, Mack said, "Well, that won't be any time soon."

Kevin stared across the parking lot, deep in thought. "Looks like you guys have a tiger by the tail. If this Archer is what the drug dealer says he is, you're up against a very dangerous person with a lot of skill, experience, and a deep bag of tricks. He may even be using federal frequencies." Kevin paused a moment, then smiled. In his usual calm and quiet-spoken demeanor, he said, "Well now, this really intrigues me. This doesn't come along every day. If you want, you have me at your disposal. I'd like a chance to prove my tricks are better than his."

Mack grinned. "All right! Good. What now?"

In a more somber tone, Kevin replied, "Now that we know that your target is a skilled electronics expert, we have a direction to follow. Your Mr. Archer has probably been listening to your conversations and knows everywhere you go. And that might go for everyone in your immediate orbit." Kevin suggested, "First, I want to run a TSCM inspection on all your offices, homes, and cars ASAP."

Mack and Bob almost said it in unison. "TSCM?"

"It stands for technical surveillance countermeasures. It's very time consuming, because I have to examine the ambient electromagnetic spectrum at all locations before the actual sweep. That way I can analyze what should be there versus what shouldn't be there. An RF spectrum analysis can't be rushed to do it right, ya know?"

Bob's eyes rolled. Mack laughed and said, "Sure, anybody knows that."

Archer spent several hours charging batteries and adjusting frequencies. He pondered, *why would the P.I. go to that prison in Rahway? Doesn't make sense. Maybe it has to do with another case he's working on.* GPS monitoring of Mack's Range Rover was working fine. It just hadn't produced much of value to Archer yet. Comparing the navigation receiver's incoming coordinates with a Google map, he thought, *Now he's at the grocery store. Pretty mundane for a big-shot private eye. Patience, Ted, patience.* He sat back in the man cave and plotted his next move. *The diary!*

Chapter *Twenty-Two*

Archer parked **50 yards from the Lott home,** almost invisible in the darkness against some trees and large shrubbery. At 3:45 a.m., the streets were dead quiet. Before starting his mission, he sat in the mini-van for about 40 minutes checking the Lott home and its surrounding neighborhood. He looked for a light going on or off, a glowing cigarette, or any movements indicating someone up and around. Nothing. His previous surveillance efforts had not revealed the presence of dogs in the Lott home nor in any of the close neighbors. Archer alighted stealthily from the mini-van, its inner light bulbs previously removed for security.

If I can just get this window jimmied without making noise. There! He pulled himself over the sill and into the Lott kitchen. The six-watt nightlight over the sink enabled him to orient himself before starting his search for the diary.

"Who's there!" Melanie Lott reached for the flashlight next to her bed and began to yell at the top of her voice. "Mark, someone's in the kitchen. I saw a shadow. Come quick!"

In less than 30 seconds Archer shimmied back out the window, closed it, and sprinted to the mini-van. He did a quick U-turn and sped away. *Damned nightlight! I shoulda clicked it off and used my night vision.* He hadn't known about Melanie Lott's back condition and that she slept in her dining room in a hospital bed, cursed with fitful sleep.

"Mother, there's no one here. You were dreaming." Mark yawned, shook his head, slowly ascended the stairs and returned to bed.

"I saw a shadow. It moved." She yelled after him. She muttered, "I wasn't dreaming, dammit!" Melanie turned on her reading light. She stared at the kitchen door until her eye-lids gave in to a restless slumber. When dawn broke through the dining room blinds, Melanie was snoring and clutching her flashlight.

Archer was still angry with himself, as he sipped his second cup of coffee in the all-night diner. *Gotta figure out another way to get my hands on that diary.* At dawn, he drove back to the Lott neighborhood and slowly glided down the street. He clicked the bug's receiver on and heard Melanie

Lott's gentle snoring. Still pissed, he glanced at the Lott house, sneered and sped off. *At least the bug I slapped under the kitchen counter works.*

Back at his man cave, Archer had been pecking away on the computer for the last hour. The only sounds heard were his finger-taps and the occasional clicking noises from the minivan, its engine heat still dissipating.

"Ah-hah! Here it is." He finally hacked his way into Somerset Hospital's patient record system. What he found would please McGinn and ease Alfred Stewart's concerns. He spun around on his high-top chair and stepped over to the small refrigerator for a Michelob. He snickered condescendingly, "How 'bout that, she spent time in the psyche ward. That should keep 'em happy for a while."

Every member of the team was crowded into attorney Reddy's small conference room: Mack, Bob, Maria and Jose Rodriguez, Mark Lott, Julie Owens, and Penny. Reddy agreed to have his office used as a safe place to conduct business after Kevin Murray ran a sweep and gave the all-clear for listening devices.

Bob couldn't help himself as he wiggled his chair, trying to get a couple inches closer to the table. "After we bring ABP to its knees with a large settlement, Avery, I hope you'll be able to afford a real conference room."

Mack gave him a serious and semi-annoyed look and said, "We wanted to bring everyone together because we all need to be on the same page about some very important stuff. We're lucky to have one of the top electronic surveillance guys on the planet as part of our team. This is Kevin Murray and I want everyone to listen carefully to what he has to say."

"Thanks for the introduction, Mack. Folks, I am here today to warn you about something that's intended to undermine what you're trying to do. Actually, something we found yesterday confirms that you are really onto something." Kevin paused, now that he had everyone's attention. "Yesterday, I conducted an electronic search and found that Mack's Range Rover not only has a listening device connected to it, but I also found an illegal GPS sending unit."

Deep frowns all around and a shared murmur resulted. Kevin slowly nodded his head, as he went on.

"We suspected something like this could come up, because of what we found out about the guy who Mack has identified."

Mack interrupted, "We'll need to check all your homes and cars to be sure they haven't been bugged. But the main thing to remember: once we find a listening device, we'll leave it in place. We're gonna use the bugs to our advantage—if we get the opportunity—by feeding the other side misleading information."

Kevin continued, "Mack will set up appointments for me to visit with you. But remember, it's crucial that no one talks about this to anyone, especially in your home or car before I have a chance to check them out carefully. While I'm at your places, there will be no discussions, either. Now, there's more. Your phones are likely bugged, also. Bob is passing out special cell phones with chargers for you to use during this time period. And this is very important. You should use them only for contacting Mack and Bob and only when outside your car and away from the house."

Mack finished up. "I know this is difficult. It is a violation of your privacy, but we have to do this to protect you and to catch the killers of Henry Lott and those who caused the death of Sofia Rodriguez. If we are to get the upper hand in this investigation, we need your full and airtight cooperation."

It was barely a whisper, but Mark Lott's remark was loud enough to be heard. "Oh, crap!"

Mack caught it. "What?"

Mark said, "I don't know if it means anything, but my mom thought she saw someone in the kitchen in the middle of the night. I told her she was dreaming and went back to bed. But now I'm not so sure." He spoke to Kevin. "Can you start with our house?"

As the office cleared out, Kevin directed his final comments to Mack and Bob. "I think you both should rent alternative vehicles for the time being. But we do have an opportunity here to feed bad intel to Archer, should he be listening. And you two would be his best targets. So, give some thought to trying phony conversations in your own vans in case he is listening. It's worth a try."

Reddy patted Mack on the back as he and Bob were the last to leave the conference room. "Mack, you guys are on the right track. But don't underestimate this Archer guy. He is obviously ruthless and knows what he's doing."

"We know, Avery. We're a step ahead of him knowing about the bugs. We'll be playing him now."

"By the way, I filed Sofia's law suit against ABP this morning. That should tick things up a notch at their end."

Bob winked at Mack and said, "So, at Heaven's Gate, St. Peter looked at his book and back at the lawyer. 'Forty years old, you say? According to your billing records, you should be 83.'"

Avery feigned going ballistic. "Get him outta here." He shouted, "Janice, where's my gun?"

Chapter *Twenty-Three*

Wendy rolled over, away from McGinn, hugging a pillow. She wasn't sure how to broach the subject. *Something bad is going on and I bet that Archer is in the middle of it. He scares me.* She sighed deeply.

"What's with you, today?" McGinn sensed her edginess.

"Oh, I don't know." She turned back and said, "I guess I'm a little jumpy with all this tension goin' on at work. Ever since that woman killed herself—and that happening right after Henry's accident—I don't know. It's all so creepy, so unnerving."

McGinn reached over to hold her closer. "You worry too much. I'm taking care of all that. Besides, I've just learned that woman's death had nothing to do with the drug trial. She spent time in a psychiatric ward. She was a nut case and shouldn't have been part of the test group, anyway." He stroked Wendy's hair, smiled, and said, "Hey, we're not here to talk business."

But she persisted. "Poor Alfred. He seems so upset that the trial may be at risk. That's another thing. What about all the work and expense that went into the new drug? Is that all down the drain?"

"We're working on that. Not to worry." McGinn's irritation level was rising.

Wendy paused a long moment. Pushing further, she asked, "And what's Archer got to do with all this?"

McGinn tensed up. He pulled away from her and threw his legs over the edge of the bed. "Archer!" He spoke the name disdainfully. "Why mention him?"

"There *is* something with him, Peter. I just know it. Who is he, really? What has he done? You two always look like you're scheming behind closed doors."

McGinn got up and started dressing. "I don't want to talk about this."

"And I still don't understand what that private detective was getting at. He said, 'If it was an accident.'" Wendy was on all fours on the bed. "What did he mean by that, Peter?"

"He was just talking crap, Wendy." He whipped around and leaned on the bed, pulling her head back by her hair, his face close to hers. "I told you I was handling it."

"Stop! Peter, you're hurting me!"

McGinn grabbed her by the arm and pulled her upright, slapping her face. "Enough!" He pushed her against the headboard and held her there. "You will not mention this again, if you know what's good for you. Understand?"

Suddenly frightened, all she could do was nod her head. She was seeing a side of Peter McGinn she'd never seen before. He quickly dressed and left the hotel abruptly, leaving her in tears.

Later that afternoon, Wendy came to McGinn's office. She stood in front of his desk, the side of her face still red from his slap. "Peter, we're done. We won't be meeting again like that. And here's my resignation."

"Wendy, I'm sorry, I . . ."

"No. You don't slap me and push me around like your rag doll." She rolled back her sleeve. "You don't bruise my arm. All I wanted to do was help you, Peter. I now realize I don't even know you. I don't know what you and Archer are up to, but I'm sure I don't want anything to do with it."

"No matter what happened between us, please don't quit. I can only apologize for my bad behavior." He rose and came around from behind his desk. "Look, Wendy, this job is tough. I have to make decisions for the good of this company, and sometimes the pressure gets to me."

Wendy stepped back and away, a look of disgust on her face. "I'm no longer interested in your problems, *Doctor* McGinn. The only way I'm staying on is if you stay totally away from me except to check on data and give me two new people for my section. We're behind since Henry's death and I need to get caught up. And I need them now and I need to start interviewing right away. Right away!" Wendy's air of haughty indifference sealed the end of their personal relationship. It would be all business from now on.

"Very well." McGinn sighed. "See to it, then. Check with personnel and place the usual ads. I'm busy right now." McGinn directed his attention back to the papers on his desk. Wendy abruptly turned around and left the office. McGinn walked slowly to the window and stared out at the geese floating tranquilly on the pond below and thought, *I hope she stays out of the way, for her sake.*

Archer removed his headphones and bit his lower lip. *I knew that bitch would be a problem.* He started the minivan and pulled slowly out of the employee parking lot.

It was close to midnight when Wendy finished her shower. Her hair was wrapped in a towel when the doorbell rang. She opened it, but just to the length of the chain. Archer's full weight against the door ripped screws loose and knocked Wendy to her vestibule floor.

Archer stood over her and slammed the door behind him. "You and I are gonna have a little talk, Ms. Hewitt."

Wendy screamed, "Get out!." And then she screamed again.

Archer grabbed Wendy by one leg and dragged her into the next room. "Shut up." Her robe fell away exposing her nakedness.

Wendy panicked. "Don't!"

Archer leered at her, but said, "Don't worry, bitch, I'm not interested in you." With his right hand, he brutally grabbed both sides of her face, distorting it as he squeezed. "Now you listen and you listen good. Your little 'Peterkins' and I are doing business and you're not gonna fuck it up. Am I getting through to you?"

Wide-eyed and in pain, she could only blink quickly. Archer went on. "Your ass is on the line, too. You are the one who was pushing on Henry. You will go to work tomorrow like nothing happened, right? And keep your mouth shut or I'll shut it!"

"Umm." His grip was so tight, she couldn't speak. He released her face with a disgusted shove.

With a sinister half-smile, Archer said, "It wouldn't look good to have more bodies piling up, if you catch my drift." With that, he left, slamming the door hard behind him.

Chapter *Twenty-Four*

Alfred Stewart summoned McGinn to his office. "Peter, I am very worried. We were served this morning with a lawsuit accusing us of causing that woman's suicide by rushing the trial forward without proper review.

"Alfred, I am concerned, too, and I can assure you that woman who killed herself had mental issues going into the trial and . . ."

Alfred interrupted scornfully. "That's no answer. Doesn't every person with dementia have mental issues going into drug trials?"

"What I mean is, she shouldn't have been chosen for other reasons. I'm working with our lawyers to get all the facts and come up with a good defense, Alfred."

"This is very distressing, Peter. This could damage us very much. We have to stay ahead of it and we have to sort it out so we can protect ourselves and still do the right thing. I want you to keep me in the loop on this every day.

On another subject, you know my family's history. You remember the stories about my grandfather—I call him Alfred the First." Stewart managed an affectionate smile and continued. "We're about to follow in his footsteps. I've just agreed to join in with Arthenta Pharmaceuticals on a shared research project. They've come up with a new approach for destroying cancer cells by getting the cells to turn on each other. It's all very hush-hush right now."

McGinn made light, "So it's a kind of a cannibalism party for cancer cells?"

"It's no joke, Peter. The lawyers are working out the details, as we speak. I already have their proprietary formula in the company safe." He jerked his head toward the portrait of Grandpa Stewart over the fireplace. "For your information, that formula is still a secret and could be worth a lot of money on the black market, so keep this under your hat." Alfred's body language conveyed the meeting was over, and McGinn took the cue.

Hmm. A secret formula. Right here in the safe. McGinn smiled all the way back to his office.

Nezzie answered the phone, "Mackey Investigations, how can we help you?" Nezzie could tell there was someone at the other end, but all she heard was breathing. "Okay, wise guy, be that way." She pulled the headset from her ear, but before she could hang up, she heard a woman's voice.

"Hello?"

"Yes. Who's calling?"

"I need to speak with Mr. Mackey."

Nezzie thought, *Me too, dearie. He hasn't checked in with me yet this afternoon.* "He's not in right now. Can I tell him what this is about?"

"No, uh, maybe I'll call back."

"Well, at least give me your name." Nezzie leaned into the phone sensing the woman was stressed.

"Wendy Hewitt." She hung up without a good-bye.

Considering the way Wendy retreated into her condo the last time they met, Mack thought it best to bring Penny along to soften her anxiety.

"Mack, check out the door frame." Penny said cautiously, "Something happened here."

"Yeah. Let's find out."

Not really surprised to see Mack at her door, Wendy greeted them and walked toward her living room with her head down. Wringing her hands and obviously nervous, she opened the conversation. "Thanks for coming. I did want to talk to you, Mr. Mackey. Things have changed since the last time we met." She began to sob. "I'm so scared. I don't know what to do."

Penny moved closer and took Wendy's hands. "We're here to help." She looked to Mack for follow up.

"It's Ted Archer, isn't it?"

Wendy stopped crying. "How did you . . ."

"Ms. Hewitt, we've been conducting an investigation into Henry's death. We believe he was murdered and that ABP is involved. Now that we know Archer is on the scene, it's pretty clear he had to be the hit man. Besides, the condition of your front door makes me think you had a visit from him. Am I right?"

"Murder? Henry was murdered?"

"It sure looks that way, almost positive. We believe his car was tampered with, causing the accident."

"Oh God. Oh my God! And Peter is involved. That's what's wrong with him."

"You mean Peter McGinn, the vice president."

"Yes. He and I were . . . I mean, he was . . ."

"We know that, too. The reason we came without calling is we don't trust the phones. Archer has been planting listening devices. Hopefully, he doesn't have one here yet." Mack looked around anxiously.

"Last night he broke in here and pushed me to the floor. He threatened me. I was terrified." Wendy couldn't sit still. She walked back and forth with her arms tight across her breasts and her shoulders hunched.

"He said I had to go to work today and act as if nothing happened. I did go in, but I was terrified every time I turned around. He also said something like, 'can't have bodies piling up.' I didn't sleep at all last night. I'm so scared and I don't know what to do next. That's why I called you."

"You could report the attack to the police. But that wouldn't help us put him behind bars for Henry's murder." Mack prompted Penny with a look. "There could be another way."

Penny said, "Mack and I were talking about it as we came over here. If there were a way we had someone on the inside of ABP who could provide us with information, our case would stand a better chance."

"You mean me? I don't see what I could do. I've already done way too much." Wendy, suddenly looking weak, collapsed on her sofa and started sobbing.

"I can't believe I was so blind and now Henry's dead and I am part of it."

Penny slipped onto the sofa and put her arm around Wendy. "Hey, love is blind. You had no idea what was going on. You're a victim in this, too."

Still reeling from knowing that McGinn and Archer were involved in Henry's murder, she shook her head and said, "What on earth did I see in that man?"

Wendy started sobbing again, "I can't believe I put so much pressure on poor Henry. I can't believe he's dead."

Penny glanced quickly at Mack then said, "Hey, don't beat yourself up. If you knew what they were doing, you wouldn't have gone along."

"I'm such a sucker. He was charming and smart, and I fell for it."

Penny looked into Wendy's wet eyes and said, "Yeah, but not smart enough. We can set things right with your help. We really need your help, Wendy. Will you help us?"

Wendy took a deep breath. She felt comforted by Penny, enough to see clearly what she had to do. "Yeah. Okay, I'll do what I can. I owe it to Henry . . . and to Julie."

Showing a surprising reservoir of strength, Wendy made a weak attempt at humor, "If I don't show up tomorrow, Archer will kill me anyway."

"Not if we have anything to say about that, Wendy." Mack said, nodding at Penny.

The next morning Penny, Maria and Wendy invaded Mack's office like a D-day assault. Mack was under siege. "It's out of the question. Too dangerous. You're underestimating this guy. If Archer makes you, no telling what he'll do."

Maria said, "Look Mack, with Julie guiding us from outside, and Wendy providing opportunities inside, we might be able to find Henry's notes. You said those notes were the key to shutting down ABP and its altered drug trial. Wendy said she was approved to hire two more lab techs. We're nurses. If we can't fake chemistry class, we should hang up our stethoscopes."

Penny proposed, "And you could keep Bob Higgins in the parking lot with a signal-type thingy we could push if things turn ugly."

Mack did an eye-roll and looked to Bob for support. But Bob had a practical view of the proposal. "Actually, Mack, do you have a better idea? This trio could work pretty good together in there. And if they locate Henry's real notes, well . . ." He let the idea hang out there and tilted his head.

It wasn't that Mack didn't have confidence in them as women. He was haunted by visions of Margaret, his late wife, as she lay dying of cancer. Since then he was risk averse when it came to someone he cared about. *I can't go through that again. If I should lose Penny . . ."*

Wendy clinched it. "I have to get back there before Archer knows I stepped out, so I'll be quick. Look, there's no reason for Archer to be in the lab. It's at the opposite end of the plant from the executive offices. I think with the three of us as a team it could work."

With no other ideas on the table, Mack caved in. "Okay, but only with Bob right there in the parking lot. I guess Kevin might have a "thingy" you could use to push the alarm button," he said with a sour face. "Check with him on that, will ya Bob? And, mace, Bob, get some mace."

Chapter *Twenty-Five*

Avery Reddy climbed up the path from the 18th green at Echo Lake Country Club and headed for the bar. Echo Lake is Westfield's exclusive golf club community, home to most prominent town folks, including many members of the Union County Bar Association. After a disappointing round, Avery had little patience for Sid Nash and his usual wise cracks, but he would suffer through.

"Afternoon, Avery. Good round?"

"Hi Sid. Nah, still pulling to the left."

"That's what liberals do—pull to the left, right?"

"Funny." Avery laughed. Sid was a ball-buster from way back in their law school days together. After setting his bag down near the door, he sidled up to the bar next to his old classmate and ordered a Bloody Mary.

Nash, never short of jibes for fellow lawyers, said, "By the way, scuttlebutt is your case against the pharmaceutical company is unraveling. Looks like your dead plaintiff has a psycho history. Can't be helpful."

"Whoa. Where did you hear that?"

"Hey, court houses are like sieves, baby. Just saying."

Losing confidence, he thought out loud, "I'm not sure it's worth it to keep going with this lawsuit." Attorney Reddy said, "Maria, you should have told me. This weakens our case against ABP. Your mother's breakdown and her time in the psychiatric ward will come out. The defense will say she was a poor candidate for the drug trial. They will blame you for holding back that information to get her admitted to the program." Avery slouched down in his chair and nervously waggled his pen between thumb and forefinger.

Maria's reply was caustic and without apology. "Mr. Reddy, our mama was solid up until the dementia started last year. When our papa died five years ago, it hit her hard. They were married almost 40 years. They were soul mates. They grew up in the Medellin ghetto together and climbed out of that life. It took them three years to come here legally." Maria's anger was on the rise. "How dare anyone suggest that she was unstable just because she was depressed over papa's death years ago! That's not right."

Impressed with Maria's spirited comeback, Avery rethought it. "Well, all right. It's an obstacle but we'll just have to face that head-on." He put on his "pander-to-the-jury hat" for a moment. He was coming around to Maria's argument.

Now animated, he said, "You'll need to fill me in on those details when the time comes. There's nothing like that kind of story to tug at the jury's heartstrings. In the meantime, I need your authorization to order Sofia's hospital records properly. Please sign here, at the bottom." Avery was back in control, and the law suit would continue.

Relieved and calmed as she signed the form, Maria asked, "How could her medical records have come out, anyway. Aren't they sealed or something?"

"Ever hear of hacking, Maria? I'm pretty sure we'll find Ted Archer behind this, too. After all, he is ABP's hit man and knows his way around this kind of technology."

Maria nervously waited outside the glass with the intercom phone in her hand. Uncle Diego entered the visitor's room and gave a sad, half-smile when he saw her. As tough and callous as he could be to the world, he always felt a softness in his heart toward Maria. He took a seat and asked, "So, Maria, how is the case against the drug company coming?"

Maria found it so weird: *Here's my illegal drug dealing uncle in a family of otherwise legal immigrants suing a legal drug company for negligently and illegally testing a bad drug.*

"Not too well, Uncle. Remember when mama had a nervous breakdown after papa died? Someone hacked into her medical records and now it's out in the open."

Diego's face darkened and sagged as he remembered how Sofia had fallen apart when Miguel died. After a moment, however, his tough exterior was back. "What does this mean? What does the lawyer say?"

"He said it hurts the case but he's not giving up." Maria then spoke urgently to Diego. "This man, Archer. We think he hacked into mama's hospital's records. He is trouble, Uncle. What can we do about him?"

"Don't worry, child. He's got me to worry about now. Uncle Diego will see to it."

Maria left the prison feeling strangely empowered. She knew she had just put something very deadly into motion.

Archer, you don't know what you got yourself into. Uncle Diego is on your case now.

McGinn met Alfred Stewart in the company conference room. "Alfred, our worries are over. That woman who killed herself has a long history of mental instability and we found it. She was institutionalized five years ago. She had a nervous breakdown."

Stewart was relieved. "I was sure it couldn't have been our fault. After all the good work the lab has done and the excellent reports we submitted, I'm sure the clinical trial can now be resumed. I'll get right on it with the FDA." The decent man that he was, Stewart walked to McGinn's window and stared up at the sky. "Poor woman. How she must have suffered."

McGinn ignored Stewart's last comment and warned, "There's still the lawsuit to contend with, but we have an excellent defense now. Our lawyers are drawing up a motion to dismiss the case. Something will happen soon."

"That's good, Peter. You are doing a great job taking care of this business and my family's legacy. I appreciate all your efforts."

McGinn studied the senior man leaving the room. *You better believe it. I'm the best thing this company has and when I have your job, you'll be joining your ancestors on the wall, you old fool.*

Chapter *Twenty-Six*

our occupants sat patiently in a dark green van in the ABP employee parking lot. They made no small talk. They took turns—two-by-two—watching through the one-way darkened rear window, occasionally passing binoculars back and forth. They were young men, but their youthful appearance did nothing to diminish the seriousness of their mission.

A fifth member of the group, a Suzuki Hayabusa motorcyclist, feigned engine trouble a quarter mile away. He couldn't spend too much time riding around in the near-by neighborhood without attracting attention. He appeared to be tinkering with his machine, hoping his ruse would grant him an hour or two on-site before anyone became inquisitive. His role in the operation was vital.

Archer, after a day of faking it at his ABP job, made his way to the parking lot. When his black Q-70 began to move, earbuds in the cyclist's helmet came alive. "¡Prepararse. Ahí viene!"

Archer made a left out of the lot and started north on Route 206, intending to return to his New Brunswick man cave. He passed the cyclist, gave him a casual once-over, and thought nothing more of it. But the cyclist jumped on his crotch-rocket, started it and accelerated quickly. He matched Archer's speed, hanging back about 50 yards. To Archer, there was something in the cyclist's bearing that implied urgency: *If he worships speed and noise so much, why hasn't he passed me by now? Plenty of room to pass. He just hangs back there. Something isn't right.*

Archer kept eyeing his rear-view mirror. When the green van appeared in the distance, he recognized the set up: *Classic South American assassination squad. The cycle to identify me and maybe spray lead through my driver's window. The van to finish me off and back up the biker.* Archer kept his cool. He could feel his entire body instinctively tighten and focus. He'd been here before. Continuing to drive on, he saw the traffic light ahead turn yellow, then red.

He slowed the Infiniti gradually, allowing the cyclist to come up on his left. He noticed the van had shortened the distance between them, too, but was still hanging back. When the cyclist came up almost parallel to the Infiniti, its rider glanced at the photo taped to his left wrist and turned his head to look at Archer.

It took just three seconds. Archer slammed on his brakes. The cyclist had to do the same but couldn't react quickly enough. He skidded to a stop near the Infiniti's left front bumper. Archer floored it and swerved hard slamming into the cyclist with the left corner of the Q-70, dislodging him from the bike and sending him tumbling into the path of a left-turning mattress truck. A set of double-axle rear tires finalized Archer's efforts when they ran over the cyclist's head.

Archer accelerated suddenly through the red light and drove forward about 200 feet past the intersection. The van tried to keep up. Archer timed it perfectly. He threw the car into neutral, engaged the parking brake, and spun the wheel hard to the left. The 3,800-pound luxury vehicle nimbly turned completely around amid the screeching of smoking tires. Archer nudged the still-sliding car flawlessly into southbound traffic. He laughed tauntingly into the shocked face of the van driver, as he flashed by in the opposite direction. Racing through a corner gas station, his Q-70 sped westbound away from pursuers onto secondary roads through rural farmland.

Several minutes into his flight, Archer pulled off onto a dirt road and came to a stop in a wooded glade, several hundred feet from the road. He inspected the damage to the front of the car and found it to be negligible.

In the distance, sirens blared as he opened the trunk to retrieve his backup kit: food, water, toiletries, and a change of clothes—everything he would need until early the next morning. With his frenzied escape over, he had time for the pressing question: *Who just tried to kill me? Hispanics, for sure. You weren't the first and you probably won't be the last, amigos. But who and why?*

He stripped back the lining on the right side of the trunk and retrieved a 15-round nine-millimeter Glock 23. He pulled back on the slide a half-inch or so to confirm a round in the chamber, engaged the safety and stuffed the hefty automatic into his waistband. *Try that again, muchachos and the body count will be more than one!*

Chapter *Twenty-Seven*

For the benefit of others in Human Resources** who might be listening, Wendy Hewitt introduced herself to the newly arrived hires. "Pleased to meet you both. Welcome to Analytic Bio-Pharm. Let me show you to your lockers and introduce you to your co-workers in the laboratory." She walked ahead of Maria and Penny, guiding them down the hall toward the lab.

There was no conversation out of the ordinary, only a knowing look that passed between them. After work, they would meet and talk at Mack's office to review the day's activities, but not before.

Mack asked, "How's it coming, Kevin?"

"Shouldn't be long now. I'm just about to test this out with one of my own demonstration listening devices." Kevin cleared the office for bugs and was setting up a jamming device intended to make Mack's office safe against electronic intrusion.

Nezzie answered the phone and signaled Mack to pick up. She whispered, "Your detective friend from Union County."

Mack nodded and picked up. "Hey Bill. How's things in the big city?"

Chief of County Detectives William Worten and Mack were partners almost 20 years ago in the Union County Prosecutor's Office. They stayed in touch. "All good, Mack. You?"

"Good." After a long pause, Mack said, "Okay, I'll bite. You never call me socially, so what's on your little defective detective mind today?"

"I'm just giving you a heads up. I don't know if it means anything to you or not. I was at a narcotics joint task force meeting in New Brunswick this morning and had an interesting conversation with a Somerset gang unit guy. He was called in on an auto accident on Route 206, because the fatal was a MS-13 kid. It seems there was a wild incident involving a car, a cycle, and a van. Witnesses said the guy in the car was the target of a hit, but the tables turned and the biker went down. The car and van both skedaddled in different directions. The only reason I'm calling you on this is that a detective heard you had been in headquarters to talk to them about a pharmaceutical company that might be involved in murder. The incident happened to take place just a mile or so from ABP Pharma. He thought it coincidental but worth mentioning. Mack, you and I know there are no coincidences, right?"

"Right. No coincidences, and none with this one, either. You've made my day, Bill. Thanks for the call."

"Whoa, hold up a minute. Don't I get a little bit back?"

Mack filled Worten in on the case and asked him to keep it under his hat for now. "If they wouldn't listen to me before—over there in Somerset—they won't listen now. I know who was driving the car and I know who set up the hit. I'll keep you in the loop, pal. Thanks again."

"Hey, it's not my jurisdiction, anyway. Need anything, just call. Good luck, bud."

Archer was puzzled. He knew there were many who wanted him dead, especially in South America, but he doubted they could find him and then line up a hit that easily. Taking an analytical approach, he thought, *they tailed me from the*

company parking lot. That was their starting point. But how would they know to do that?

Trained to never be reactive, his mind turned to identifying the cyclist and his van pals. He called an informant who had the right contacts in New Jersey's Hispanic circles. That was "the way to Jesus," in DEA speak. Archer knew most valuable intelligence comes from informants, whether they're paid or pressured. The mantra is: *When in doubt, find a squealer.* Or in Archer's world, *make* one squeal. And his informant, Manuel, owed Archer big time.

Manuel called back in under an hour. He reported there was a MS-13 death ritual for a fallen brother in Newark scheduled for the following night. But there was a clincher: Manuel confirmed the decedent died in a car crash not far from Somerville. Archer laughed out loud, "Gotta love talk on the street."

He parked his white minivan across from the dilapidated funeral home just off Clinton Avenue in Newark. Archer viewed the group through his night-vision binoculars as they smoked pot in front of the funeral home. He recognized the driver of the dark green van immediately.

After milling around near the curb for 20 minutes, they broke up. Archer followed the van driver home to a second-floor walk-up on Conklin Avenue in the Weequahic section of the city. He waited until close to 5 a.m., pulled on synthetic gloves, and put his plan into action. *He'll tell me what I need to know.*

"¿Como se llama?" Archer whispered the question into the kid's left ear as he lay sleeping in his twin bed. There was no answer, but Archer didn't expect one. Not yet. He wanted the seriousness of the moment to sink into the sleepy mind of his subject. Slowly releasing his strangle-grip on the frightened kid's throat, Archer emitted a low, slow "Shh! We don't want to disturb anyone else, do we?" The young wide-eyed gang member shook his head with fear-filled ferocity. "I asked a question. What's your name?"

He responded hoarsely, "Mi-Mi-Miguel." He was beginning to shake.

Archer hissed, "You know who I am, Miguelito?

The kid nodded slowly, a tear ran down his left cheek.

"Do you wish to live, Miguelito?"

With a throaty whisper, the kid said, "Si, señor!"

"Who put the hit out on me? Tell me and I will let you live. Lie to me and you are as dead as your biker friend. "¿Estás muerto, comprende?" Archer began to squeeze again. The kid waved at him to stop.

162

Chapter Twenty-Seven

Miguel murmured painfully, "Gomez. Es Diego Gomez."

"And where do I find this Gomez?"

"In Rahway Prison. But please tell no one I . . ."

Rahway. It makes sense now. That's why that damned P.I. was at the prison.

Gripped with fear, Miguel pleaded, "Please, señor, my neck!"

Archer rammed his right knee into Miguel's solar plexus and held him down. At the same time, he squeezed the boy's carotid arteries as hard as he could, rendering Miguel unconscious in several seconds. He reached into his boot and pulled out a small black case, withdrew a hypodermic syringe and shot its milky white substance into a vein in Miguel's left arm, leaving the syringe dangling there. *Everyone will think you were so upset over your buddy's death, you overdosed.*

Archer patted Miguel's flaccid face. *Sorry, kiddo, I lied.* He dropped a couple of folded packets of heroin behind the kid's bed and quietly padded out of the apartment and back to the van. *Now, to call in a marker. Rahway Prison. Shouldn't be a problem comin' up with a friend in there.*

Chapter *Twenty-Eight*

After Maria and Penny were introduced to others in the lab they began their first day at ABP. Eager to get started on their search mission, they nonetheless knew enough to act like regular employees and not arouse suspicions.

"Let's just fit in first," said Penny. "We'll take our cues from Julie."

The real job before them seemed impossible. There were innumerable drawers and shelves to search, spread over nearly a half-acre. The laboratory was overwhelming in size.

They went through their first day following others around. Though separated, Penny and Maria kept visual track of one another. Each had a pendant on a chain hanging from her neck that, when squeezed, would send an alert to Bob Higgins out in the parking lot. Each carried a small canister of mace in her lab coat, should it be needed.

As the two women moved around they kept a sharp eye out for possible places where Henry's notes might be filed away or hidden.

Archer was seated in one of McGinn's side chairs. McGinn, standing at the window, stared out at the geese, some with their tails pointing skyward as they bottom fed. Both were silent, having just discussed the attempt on Archer's life several days before.

The silence was broken by a knock on the door and Wendy entered. "You wanted to see me, Dr. McGinn?" She eyed Archer nervously. He smugly met her fleeting glance with a cold stare.

"Yes, Wendy. It seems that Henry Lott had a diary." McGinn motioned for Wendy to sit in the other side chair. He continued. "You and I know the contents of that diary could be damaging to all of us. It probably makes mention of his warnings to us about the lab animals' behavior and the like." McGinn back-tracked for a moment. "I take it you are aware of the lawsuit filed by Lott's lawyer?"

"It's all over the company, of course."

"Mr. Archer and I are looking for that diary. Any ideas?"

Wendy put on a thoughtful face. She frowned and angled her head, as if in deep thought. "No, I would have no idea where to start looking for it. Maybe he kept it at home?" *Wouldn't you love to know there is no diary, you bastards!*

Archer spoke up. "Ms. Hewitt, you worked closely with Henry, right?"

Wendy answered defensively, "I think you know I did. I was his immediate boss, but I didn't keep track of his every move."

"Uh-huh." Archer's cynical expression showed his disapproval. "Let's cut to the chase, Wendy. We all know that you were the one who ordered him to destroy his notes. You were the one who kept after him to sign off on the flawed protocol. So, you are in this up to your neck." Archer never pulled punches.

McGinn sat calmly behind his desk but couldn't make eye contact with Wendy.

Wendy responded in a pleading voice. "I only did what you told me to do, Peter." Wendy had all she could do to keep a straight face. *I'm a better actor than I thought.*

McGinn slowly nodded his head. "Yeah, and you are in this up to your neck, as Ted said."

166

Chapter Twenty-Eight

After a painful pause, Wendy pleaded, "So, what am I supposed to do now?"

McGinn started to speak, but Archer signaled him to stop.

"We want you to search the lab from top to bottom and find that damned diary. You know the ins and outs of that place better than anyone. It's your ass too, if you don't find it." He turned to McGinn and remarked, "In the meantime, Peter and I will be looking elsewhere."

As Wendy walked back down the long hallway toward the lab, she rebuked herself. Cringing, she thought, *how could I ever have let that evil shit's hands touch my body?* Turning a corner, she whispered under her breath, "How about this, Archer? Maybe I should enlist the help of the two new girls to find the diary that doesn't exist. And just maybe we might find something else. Talk about having the best cover for searching!"

That night at Mack's office, the women were almost giddy over the day's events. Mack walked in to find them all talking at once. When he learned of Archer's instructions, he laughed out loud.

Chapter *Twenty-Nine*

Diego Gomez walked across fifty yards** of well-worn concrete in the prison yard heading toward his homies. Each ethnic group—black, white, and Hispanic—ruled their own section of the prison yard. This self-imposed separation was not set up by prison officials; but was encouraged to lessen the opportunity for violence.

About midway across the yard, a tall head-shaved inmate approached from Diego's right side. He was smiling.

"Whatchu want, Anglo?" Diego recognized him as one of the White Supremacists.

At that same moment, four other white inmates started a scuffle on the opposite side of the yard. The shouting of profanity and physical shoving looked like the beginning of a fight, so a half-dozen correction officers quickly moved in to break it up.

Ignoring the fracas, the tall man drew closer to Diego and said calmly, "I have a message for you from Ted Archer."

With that, he plunged a shank twice into Diego's belly before Diego could pull himself away.

Suddenly, the prison yard erupted. Three rival gangs slammed together in the yard's center, violently savaging one another in a fight that left two dead and 30-some injured. It took two dozen officers and the use of tear gas to restore order. And amidst all the commotion, Diego lay face-down on the ground, but with enough sense to press his hand against his wounds to slow the flow of blood.

Diego's toughness served him well. After two operations, he managed to stabilize and survive. He lay recovering in the prison hospital for ten days. Lucky for Diego, the shank missed his vital organs and only ripped open muscles across his abdomen. It was extremely painful but not life-threatening.

When Archer heard Gomez was still alive, he threw his coffee cup across the man cave. *Dammit, should've known when I took this job things would somehow get fucked up. I'm not done with you yet, Gomez!*

Attorney Reddy stood up when it was his turn. "Your honor, we find the defendant's argument to be spurious and completely without merit. In addition, it is an insult to this court. To argue that a serious depression after the loss of a dearly-beloved life-companion five years earlier, would disqualify someone from entering an Alzheimer's drug trial is ridiculous. Further, to intimate that she killed herself as the result of a mental defect is outrageous. We will show that Sofia Rodriguez—a *legal* immigrant by the way, from Colombia—was fully recovered from that depression and had every right to be in the drug trial."

Opposing counsel argued that within Mrs. Rodriguez' history was a nervous breakdown that, no matter the cause or duration of elapsed time, would taint the findings of that drug trial, even if she had not killed herself. He said, "How can the plaintiff state with a straight face that his client's mental condition would have no impact on a dementia drug trial when that very drug is intended to treat a mental condition? No, your honor, we are left with a serious doubt that the drug trial played any part in the unfortunate death of Mrs. Rodriguez"

Undeterred by opposing counsel's argument, Avery gave one final push. Glaring at the other attorney and turning directly toward the judge, he said, "A serious doubt? Really? Isn't that what a trial is about? A motion to dismiss has to be much stronger than a serious doubt."

Confidence rising, he went on, "Your honor, it seems the only way to settle this is by expert testimony. I request you that postpone your decision pending review of expert-witness testimony which will show Mrs. Rodriguez had fully recovered from her episode of depression and rightfully entered the drug trial expecting to see the positive results that ABP held out as a possibility. And as it turned out, ABP appears to have failed her terribly."

The judge grudgingly concurred. "Gentlemen, your next hearing will be scheduled for about six weeks from now. My law clerk will provide you with date and time. In the meantime, you will submit written expert reports for me to consider." The judge smiled sarcastically and threw in, "This will be interesting. Neither expert will have examined the victim, yet will render a psychological opinion. I can't wait to see this, myself. This hearing is adjourned."

Wendy and Julie discussed the lab layout and possible places where Henry could have hidden his notes on 14168-ALZ. Wendy said, "The other girls and I checked all the obvious places: drawers, cabinets, shelves and even the drop ceiling. Maria almost brought the whole ceiling down when the ladder shifted."

Julie insisted, "It must be there somewhere. He said he would show me the notes on Monday when we were back at work. He must've thought something bad could happen. Otherwise, why would he hide them so well?" Julie's head lurched to one side. Her eyes narrowed. Her jaw clenched. "Wait. Something he said . . ."

Wendy watched as Julie's disposition abruptly changed. "What is it? What's the matter, Julie?" Julie was deep in thought, not in the present. She got up from Mack's conference room table and began pacing back and forth. She stopped suddenly, her hands reaching across her chest and gripping her opposing shoulders tightly.

Trying desperately to recall what happened leading up to that deadly moment, she droned on in a rhythmic voice, "We just left the restaurant. Henry repeated he was troubled that the clinical trial might start on humans." Searching for the details, she pounded her right fist into the palm of her left hand several times.

"He said something about you, Wendy." Julie froze, staring at the ceiling. "I . . . I . . . He said, 'Wendy told me to destroy my notes, but I hid them.'"

Julie spun around, looking almost stunned and leaned heavily on the conference table. She shouted excitedly, "I remember!" She drew a quick breath and held it. She threw her head back and laughed out loud. But her joy was fleeting. Her memory had returned . . . all of it. Her head dropped to her chest. Her hands dropped to her sides. She was exhausted.

Wendy came around the table to console Julie. She took her hands and said, "What is it, Julie? Tell me."

Julie was barely able to get it out. She whispered, "Henry winked at me. He said, 'It's a puzzle. I'll show you Monday. It's *food for thought*.'"

Nodding her head repeatedly and in a quiet voice, slowly said, "I think I know where the notes are, Wendy. Henry always used the words *food for thought w*hen he fed the lab rats. Get it? Food for the rats in exchange for *thought*. Thought, as in dementia patients. He was always saying clever things like that, but that one was his favorite."

She leaned toward Wendy. "The notes are with the rat food. I'd bet on it. Somehow, they have to be with the rat food." Emotionally drained, she reached for Wendy and began to cry. Her words came out rapid-fire. "It just came back to me. I remembered. I remembered. The accident. It was so awful! I thought I died there with Henry." Julie sobbed uncontrollably. Her voice trailed off, "Then I woke up in the hospital."

Julie collapsed into Wendy's embrace. "Get it out girl. You need this cry." Wendy laughed and whispered into Julie's ear, "Sweetie, you did it. We'll find Henry's notes now, and fix those bastards for good!"

Chapter *Thirty*

D **iego slowly entered the visitor's area,** painfully clutching his abdomen with both hands, as he moved. Their eyes met, as he shuffled toward the glass. Mack slowly shook his head back and forth, a sour frown on his face,

The convicted drug dealer spoke into the intercom with difficulty. "Whassup, Five-0?"

"Ya just couldn't resist, could ya?"

"A little birdie told me your case wasn't doin' so good. So, I did what I do. Right?"

"Wrong. The lawyer is doing his job. I'm doing my job. And *you* are screwing it up! And look at you. You're lucky to be alive."

"You 'spect me to sit in here and do nothin'? That asesino is working for the people who killed my sister. He's out front for them." Diego gathered strength, his face suddenly angry, and shouted, "They killed my sister!"

The prison guard stationed near the door dropped his folded arms and looked over, wearing an alarmed expression.

Mack waved him, a "No problem!" and shushed Diego.

Reaching beneath his gray prison tunic, Diego gently rubbed his still painful stomach. In a more subdued voice, he said, "We take care of our own, bro."

Well, from Five-0 to bro. I'm getting somewhere. Mack assumed a more tolerant attitude. "Yeah, he is an assassin. We'll be getting to him. You can count on that, *bro;* but you need to give us the time and space to get it done."

"Your way is way too slow. Too—I dunno—too mixed up with legal shit. My way is quicker and final."

"Oh yeah. How's it working for you so far, Diego? He's out there still doin' his thing and you're in here holdin' your guts in."

"Maybe so, but I ain't done yet." He grimaced and rose carefully. Standing up as straight as he could, he said dismissively, "Take a walk, Five-0. We're better at this than you are."

Penny and Maria opened the closet door where the lab rat food was stored. There were three 55-gallon drums full of brown pellets. Maria took the lid off one. "How are we going to do this, Penny? Dumping it out onto the floor is out of the question and I don't think we can reach far enough to touch bottom."

"Julie said it was probably in or *near* the rat food. Let's think about this. If Henry just shoved the notes down there in the food, he knew it could be discovered, right?"

"Right. That can't be it." Maria looked around in the cramped closet. "But there's nowhere else to hide anything."

Penny grinned. I'm not so sure." She grabbed the rim of one barrel and tried to move it. "Ugh. No go."

"Let me help." They pulled together tipping the barrel up about four or five inches. It thumped back heavily when they let go.

"Wait a minute." Maria picked up a brick acting as a temporary door stop and put it against the bottom of the barrel. "Let's try again. When we get it up, I'll kick the brick under the edge." It worked. They were able to peek under the barrel.

The first two barrels failed to yield anything but a bare floor. Under the third, however, they found a thick manila envelope with "14168-ALZ" scribbled at the top. Penny reached in, retrieved it and stood up, triumphantly announcing, "We got it!"

Archer tapped her on the shoulder. "I'll take that. You two didn't fool me. I've been watching you since you got here." Archer shot a quick glance up to the air conditioning vent and the tiny camera behind it. "Thanks for doing our work for us. Right, Wendy?"

Wendy was standing behind Archer. "Oh, absolutely, Ted."

Penny and Maria could only stare at each other, as Archer ripped the envelope from Penny's grip. Wendy stood behind Archer, wearing a blank look. Penny's face went white.

"Wendy, how could you? We trusted you."

Archer said, "Wendy knows her place and it's not with you." He turned to leave.

"Right. I know where my bread's buttered." Wendy winked at Penny and said, "Ted, there's just one more thing."

Archer turned back and said, "What's that?"

"Well, just this!" She reached up and sprayed mace directly into the tall man's face and eyes. He recoiled, slamming his back hard into the door frame. With all the anger and fury she felt toward him and toward McGinn, she kicked him in the groin as hard as she could. Twice. He slid down clutching his crotch, moaning in agony. Wendy cast an almost nonchalant look at the other two and said, "I knew there was a reason I wore boots these last few days."

Penny and Maria leaned over Archer, as he curled up in a fetal position covering his face with one hand and grasping his groin with the other. Penny jeered, "He doesn't look so tough now, does he?"

Maria sneered and said, "Uncle Diego should see this."

The mace still burning and blurring his vision and aggravating his breathing, all Archer could do was roll back and forth, his pain so intense he could not speak.

Bob Higgins was bored but anxious. He was parked in the second row, waiting for a signal he hoped would never come. Had the women summoned him, Bob was ready to charge in and back them up. Staring at the employee entrance to ABP and wondering what was going on inside, he suddenly saw the lady musketeers come flying out and immediately slow to a fast walk.

Moving briskly down the long path to the parking lot, Penny exclaimed, "Holy shit, Wendy! You're one tough cookie. Who knew?"

"Well, one guy grabs me by the hair and slaps me around. And in the same week, the other asshole breaks into my house, knocks me down, and drags me naked across the room by my ankle. Sometimes a girl's gotta do what she's gotta do. Gotta thank my Dad for those martial arts lessons when I was a kid."

"Looks like you just gave Archer a karate lesson, Wendy." Maria laughed and they all started giggling in nervous relief.

By the time the trio made it across the parking lot to Higgins' van, they were almost giddy. Penny yanked open the door and pronounced ceremoniously, "Mr. Higgins, you may remove us from this place. We have rescued piggy from the wolf."

Maria chuckled, "And the wolf is down!"

Wendy couldn't resist it. "Yeah, and he's probably licking his wounds if he can reach them."

They all howled like wolves, as Bob Higgins drove away.

Chapter *Thirty-One*

It was dark in Wendy's living room, no lights on anywhere in the condo. Mack sat on her comfy sofa, a 12-gauge shotgun cradled in his lap. Westminster chimes from the hall clock announced 3 a.m. *Nothing yet. Maybe I missed on this one. Maybe I'm wrong.* Then his Motorola portable came alive.

Bob Higgins whispered, "Action, Mack. White minivan went around the block twice, then stopped two houses down. He's out of the van, headin' your way."

Mack's answer was two clicks on his radio.

"He's on the porch. Watch yourself, pal. He's holdin.' Right hand. Looks like an automatic."

Mack heard the slight scratching sound of lock picking, then silence. The front door swung inward quickly to avoid raspy squeaks. *He's a pro. Probably wearing night vision. This will shake him up.*

Mack clicked on the 200-watt flood light and calmly said, "Hello, Ted. Don't do anything stupid. There's a 12-gauge zeroed in on your guts."

Archer drew back from the blinding light. He ripped off the night-vision goggles, his left hand shielding his eyes. He stood erect and pointed the gun at the floor. Considering the circumstances, his composure was remarkably cool. He sighed deeply. "Something told me I should've waited a while. Is that you, P.I.?"

The two men regarded each other for a moment. As Archer's vision began to come around, Mack shifted on the sofa and said, "Now, Ted, you don't want to do anything foolish. It's not like you. Why don't you put that little gun away?"

Archer hesitated. Mack continued, "Of course, I could finish the job Wendy started and blow your balls off right now." Mack laughed. "By the way, still swollen, Ted?" Mack waited several seconds then repeated harshly, "The gun!"

"For now, P.I." Archer put the pistol in his belt behind his back. He brought his right hand back slowly. He heard heavy breathing behind him and saw Higgins in the doorway with his Glock leveled appropriately. Archer sighed, "Got it covered?"

"Uh-huh. And here's how it is, asshole. We know how you killed Henry Lott. We know McGinn put you up to it. We know about the incident on 206 near the company and that Diego wants your ass dead. . ."

Archer angrily interjected, "And we both know you can't prove any of that." But he was tense, conscious of Higgins to his rear. He wasn't used to being boxed in.

Mack cocked his head and ticked off the obvious: "Let's see. I could off you right now. Think about it, Ted. You're caught breaking into the condo of a woman you beat up several days ago. You're sneaking around in the dark wearing night-vision goggles." Mack paused for emphasis, then said, "And you're carrying a piece, for Christ sake!"

"You noticed." Archer was always cool under pressure.

"Yeah. I noticed." Mack gave a heads up to Bob.

Bob got the message. He reached under Archer's jacket and retrieved the gun while keeping his own pressed against the back of Archer's head.

Tension now eased a little, Mack said, "Okay, Ted. It's crunch time. We need to make a deal. You give us McGinn and we'll give you a break, seein' as you and I are such good pals. Besides, I told Wendy I'd try not to mess up her new rug."

"What the hell is this—some kind of weird professional courtesy? How would that work? You let me leave, I'm in the wind. If you bust me, you get nothing."

"Ted, Ted. Think about it. If we bust you, you're dead meat. Your tracks are all over everything. You can think of some way to give us what we want. You're 'Mr. Resourceful,' right?"

Archer thought a moment. He looked back uneasily at Higgins again. "Okay. Okay. Here's what I can do for you. In my van there's a recording of McGinn that has what you're looking for. It's always been my insurance policy." His shoulders slumped a little, as his eyes narrowed. "Looks like it's time to cash it in for a pass." He mumbled, "I never liked that little prick, anyway."

"Hmm, if it's what you say, we have a deal. While I find it disgusting to give as pass to a scumbag like you; it's McGinn and ABP we want more than you. But you *will* leave my people alone, Ted. That includes Wendy."

Mack stood up, walked over, and got in Archer's face. "I swear. I will feed your ugly ass to sharks off the Jersey Coast if you mess with me or my people after tonight. You got it?"

As Mack stepped back, Bob Higgins joined in. "And I don't think a hungry great white would care if you were a seal or a SEAL."

Archer eyed them both cynically. "Oh yeah, I get it now. You both know you don't have enough to bust me for the lab guy. And big money goes along with grabbing McGinn and ABP, right? Right into your pockets."

"Cut the bullshit, asshole. Give Bob the keys to the van and tell him where you stashed the recording."

"How can I trust you? You could just turn around and bust me, too."

"You don't have much choice, Ted. This is the deal. I'd shake on it, but, you know."

Archer thought it over and, with a sour look of resignation, held the van keys over his head for Bob to grab.

Bob and Mack sat in Mack's car listening to the McGinn tape a second time as Archer drove off. The back and forth they heard between Archer and McGinn left no doubt about the insidious depth of the criminal conspiracy the two had hatched.

Mack said, "We have to get this to Avery. He'll see it that it makes a good case against ABP. Bob nodded in agreement but said nothing. As they drove up Route 206, the Bridgewater Diner came into view.

Bob said, "Let's have a coffee. Pull in here, Mack."

Mack always drank his black. Bob poured a little half and half into his and sat uncharacteristically quiet, stirring and sipping. Stirring and sipping. Mack noticed.

"What's up with you?"

"I guess I'm having trouble letting that psycho killer get away. We had his ass cold and now, like he said, he's 'in the wind.'"

Mack nodded and shifted in the tight diner booth. He leaned forward with his elbows on the table to emphasize his response. "I understand where you're comin' from, my friend. But the only way we were gonna nail McGinn and ABP was if Archer gave them up. Think of it as trading one dirt bag to get the one behind the whole thing.

Archer was just a means to an end for McGinn. At this point, he's the same thing for us. Besides, we're not the cops; just private investigators looking for the best way to look after our clients. Guys like Archer get theirs in the end. No worries."

"I suppose you're right, Mack. But who knows how many more will end up dead before he gets his? It still makes me queasy."

"Me too, pal. Me too. It's the business we're in."

Chapter *Thirty-Two*

Attorney Reddy was busy preparing for depositions of Alfred Stewart and Peter McGinn. Mack and Bob regularly sat in, helping to devise the best strategy for bringing out the facts and the truth.

"According to Wendy, Alfred is not likely part of the scheme to either kill Henry Lott or to put up with short-cutting the drug protocol. He's a nice old guy who takes care of his employees and guards the family legacy." Avery was setting the tone of the meeting.

Mack responded. "Nevertheless, as its president, he is responsible for what goes on in that company, right?"

"True, but we need him as an ally rather than an enemy. McGinn is the target. While we are certainly suing the company, McGinn is the bad apple. Bringing Alfred around to that thinking could be an enormous help." Avery stared an extra-long time at Mack.

"I get it. If he cooperates, and works with us, you can negotiate a settlement for the Lotts and Julie without going to trial."

"And McGinn gets turned over to the cops for the murder conspiracy. Play it again, Mack."

Mack pushed play.

Peter McGinn's voice filled the room. "We've thought it over. Warnings haven't worked, which is why you're here. We want him gone. Out of the way. Removed. Whatever way you say it."

"Damning evidence, for sure. Can you believe the unfeeling arrogance?" Avery was shaking his head, still shocked by McGinn's nonchalance after hearing the recording several times.

Bob Higgins had some doubt. "But that recording can't be used as evidence, can it? I know it's legal to record in New Jersey as long as one of the people being recorded is aware of it, but wouldn't it have to be authenticated to get into evidence? We won't have Archer to say he was the one recording it."

Avery nodded. "You're right, Bob. Legally, we can't use the recording in court. But it might be useful in another way." He looked back and forth between Bob and Mack. He tilted his head forward, and with eyebrows up, sent a "think about it" look, again, staring at Mack.

Mack caught it. "Oh yeah! Bob, Avery can't tell us, but I know what to do."

Bob, continuing his penchant for annoying Reddy, said, "Avery, what's the difference between a vulture and a lawyer?" Bob waited until Avery started to react. Then he said, "The lawyer gets frequent flyer miles."

"Mack, get him outta here!"

"Oh, I think Mr. McGinn will see me, young lady." Mack pushed the issue. "Tell him that Ted Archer sends his regards."

The receptionist gave Mack an annoyed look and got back on the phone. "I'm sorry, Dr. McGinn, but he's persistent. I'm supposed to say, 'Ted Archer sends his regards.'" After a few seconds, she hung up, continuing her frown. "Mr. McGinn's secretary is on her way down to get you."

"Now what, Mr. Mackey?" Peter McGinn was terse, his annoyance unmistakable.

"Dr. McGinn, we have Henry Lott's notes. You know that, because Ted Archer told you. Wendy Hewitt will testify that you pushed her to rush the drug protocol and to force Henry Lott to falsify his lab notes. Julie Owens will testify about her conversations with Henry. Oh, yes, and let's not forget the so-called 'accident.' You remember that, don't you?" Mack walked over to the window and looked out at the geese. They were placidly floating on the pond, not a care in the world. He turned around and said, "But it wasn't an accident, was it, Peter."

"I don't know what you're talking about." McGinn was rattled. He sat down behind his desk. "You should leave. You are misinformed. Get out!"

"Your friend, Ted Archer, ratted you out, Peter. We know you hired him to kill Henry."

McGinn shot up out of his chair. "That's absurd. Ridiculous! I did no such thing." He walked over to the bar and poured himself a scotch. "I hired Archer to warn Lott, that's all. It was to make him realize it was in his best interest to speed up his work. Henry was slow. He needed a little convincing to get the clinical trial moving along."

"Nice try, Peter. Archer never trusted you. Remember this?"

Mack reached into his pocket and pressed play. McGinn was dumbstruck. His face paled. He gulped deeply.

"You're done, Peter. You'll be lucky to get off with life." Mack turned and walked out,

McGinn slumped into his executive chair and sat rocking, his methodical mind weighing his options, sweat soaking through his Brioni dress shirt. *Be calm. Make sure you have what you need. Don't be stupid.*

He tried calling Archer on the throw-away phone but it just rang. He panicked. *I'd better get away while I still can.* He had to wait almost an hour until Alfred and his secretary left for the day then put his escape plan into motion. McGinn pulled the right side of the old portrait away from the wall over the fireplace. It turned on its hinges, revealing the rectangular wall safe. McGinn knew the combination, having watched over the old man's shoulder when he needed cash for expenses.

From the employee parking lot, Archer clicked off the bug's receiver and observed McGinn get into the Volvo, first dropping a bag behind the driver's seat. He studied McGinn's demeanor. *He's shitting in his pants. Panicking. That recording really shook him up. I knew the punk would run given the slightest push.* He followed McGinn home.

"Goin' somewhere, Peter?" Archer stood in the garage doorway, just as McGinn got out of his Volvo. Archer reached up and pushed the button on the door frame. The overhead door went down.

"Ted, let me explain . . ."

Chapter *Thirty-Three*

One week later

Mack was on his way back to ABP** to speak to Alfred Stewart when Reddy called. "Mack, I think Peter McGinn took off. I tried serving him with a subpoena for deposition—both at home and work—but he's nowhere to be found."

"No surprise there, Avery. I'm stopping in to see the president of ABP. While I'm there, I'll see if he knows where McGinn is. I'll get back to you."

Stewart, slightly built to begin with, had tired eyes and a sad haggard look. "Please come in, Mr. Mackey. I'm so glad to see you. We have quite a mess here. Dr. McGinn has absconded with cash, corporate stock and a secret formula owned by another company." He shook his head in disbelief.

"I trusted him. I can't believe it. He seemed to be doing a great job, now this. What the hell has happened?"

"I'm truly sorry for your situation, Mr. Stewart. I researched you and your company's history, so I'm pretty sure you had nothing to do with McGinn and his actions. But I'm not sure you are aware of the extent of what was going on." They settled down into Stewart's office.

"There's more?"

With company founder Alfred S. Stewart's eyes in the overhead painting staring down on the two of them, a scandal more painful than anything the Stewart family or the company had ever experienced was about to come crashing down on his grandson, Alfred S. Stewart, III.

"Well sir, Dr. McGinn hired Ted Archer to take care of the person who stood in the way of granting approvals for the trial to go forward. You recall the accident when Henry Lott, one of your employees, lost his life."

"Yes. A tragedy."

"I'm sad to have to tell you that McGinn hired Ted Archer to do away with him when he resisted major efforts to change his lab reports. McGinn thought Henry was about to be a whistleblower, which would have put a huge monkey-wrench into the Alzheimer's drug trial, so Archer rigged Lott's car to crash, and killed him."

"You can't mean they conspired to actually *murder* Henry Lott. Not Peter!" Stewart was bewildered. He thought a few seconds more, putting two and two together. "What you are saying is the protocol we submitted to the FDA was false? A fraud? Oh, my God." Alfred Stewart, III—third generation bio-entrepreneur—looked up at the painting, his most cherished connection with the past. Finally, he had to look away feeling weak and a deep sense of shame.

"And I believe you had no part in this, Mr. Stewart. The thing is, I shouldn't even be talking to you because you're represented by counsel in the family's lawsuit and I'm on the other side." Mack spoke earnestly in a subdued tone. "So, I would appreciate you keeping this conversation to yourself. As I see it, the real trial, if you'll pardon me, is how to set this right. After you've had some time to think about this, because of who you are, you'll do the right thing by those who were harmed, whatever that is. I know you will."

Stewart was silent for a very long time, rubbing his head, lost in thought. Mack sat quietly, giving him time. Finally, he said, "That's all well and good, Mr. Mackey, but I have an even bigger problem. We desperately need what McGinn stole returned—especially the secret formula entrusted to me by a colleague at another company. We have to have it back. Can I hire you to do that?"

"I'll have to check with our attorney on that one, Mr. Stewart. Because, technically, you and I are on opposite sides in the family's law suit, sir, and it would be a conflict of interest."

"Okay, but what if I were to make a quick settlement with your attorney? Could you help me then?"

Relieved, Mack smiled. "Could be, Mr. Stewart, could be."

Mack left Alfred Stewart crest fallen, staring sadly up at his grandfather's portrait.

Mack thought, *He's a quick thinker, but I can only imagine what's going through his mind. Betrayal is a hard pill to swallow.*

Bob Higgins called, very excited. "Did ya hear the latest, Mack? McGinn was found dead in his garage with his wrists slit. The cops are treating it as a suicide, but you and I know better. Wait a minute, I gotta pull over to talk. Traffic on Route 80 is nuts today."

"Yeah, Nezzie called me a few minutes ago. Who would that be? Basking Ridge PD?"

"Yup. I'll catch you there?"

The two friends were met by Detective Marty Zoke.

"Listen, guys, without anything else to go on, we're calling this one a suicide. The guy lived alone and—after I talked to his boss at the pharmaceutical company—it seemed pretty clear he offed himself after absconding with company loot."

Mack and Bob shared a knowing look. Mack asked, "Did Mr. Stewart tell you anything else?"

"Oh, so you know him. Nice old guy. Yeah, he gave me a cockamamie story about the guy murdering another employee so a drug trial could begin or something to that effect. He sounded a little around the bend, if you ask me."

Bob Higgins cranked it up a notch. "Did ya find the company loot?"

"No, that's the strange part. We searched the car, the garage and the rest of the house, but there was no bag of goodies. Hey, maybe he put it in a deposit box or something. Who knows? Anyway, our part's over. We're done. Case closed!"

Bob began to protest, but Mack cut in. "Nah. You're probably right. Another corporate suit caught with his dick in the till. Serves him right. C'mon, Bob. We got other work to do."

The two sat in Bob's van. Mack murmured the obvious, "Archer." He turned to Bob and asked, "Ever hear of anyone slitting his wrists after making a clean getaway, especially with all that money and a secret formula? It doesn't compute."

"I know. But what's Archer up to now? He knows Gomez isn't through with him. If I were him, I'd take the loot and leave the country."

"But you aren't Archer, Bob. He has a mile-high ego and he knows Diego Gomez would hunt him down all the way to Tanganyika and back before giving up. No, the fat lady ain't sung yet, pal. He's here. No matter what Zoke says, this case ain't closed, not by a long shot."

Chapter *Thirty-Four*

Archer sensed it was time to move his man cave. He knew the mainstay of good security is to be one step ahead of danger. But where to go? To pull off his next move, he would need a place somewhat remote, yet close to major roads and airports. Studying a New Jersey map and consulting Google Earth, he decided on Bayonne's waterfront.

With the help of a realtor, he located a non-descript warehouse along the Hudson River that fit his needs. Traffic was light and neighboring warehouses were empty. Anyone lingering in the area would stand out—just what Archer needed. The office was up a set of metal stairs that looked out over what decades before had been a large staging area for pallets laden with export merchandise. It had a back exit if needed. The place was old and had fallen into disrepair, but it was a perfect place to hide out.

He negotiated a one-year lease using one of his fake identities. When the facility's owner wanted to know how his tenant would be using his property, Archer's realtor assured him the products that would pass through were non-flammable, non-caustic, and consisted of dry goods imported from Malaysia.

Archer began setting up his new man cave. He planted warning devices in and around the building. He set up cameras and tested his drones for safe flight paths around the neighborhood. As before, he had an internet reception problem, so he installed a small and inconspicuous antenna on the metal roof. Things were beginning to shape up, and a time for action had arrived.

Attorney Reddy was perplexed, but pleased. "Wow. What did you say that brought him to the table so quickly?"

Mack drummed his fingers on the conference table. "Incentive is a wonderful thing, Avery. The man's whole existence is that family company. In a way, it's his Achilles' heel, too. He'd walk a mile on hot coals to save it. I merely enlightened him and he saw the big picture. So, I take it he accepted your offer to settle?"

"Not only that, he went overboard. He offered to do whatever necessary to make things right with Maria, Jose, Mark, and Julie, including withdrawing the proposed Alzheimer's drug from clinical testing until he's totally convinced it's safe to move forward. I ran that by my clients and every-one believed that the testing should continue—with the proper research protocol, of course They all said it was too important and promising, but had to be done right."

Mack thought a moment and said, "I guess now's as good a time as any to spring this on you, Avery. Alfred Stewart wants to engage us to find Archer and get back the stolen stock certificates and—most importantly—the secret formula that was in his safe-keeping." Mack sat back with a satisfied expression. "He also wants us to handle all his security and investigative needs in the future. Looks like I have a new corporate client. Go figure. Do you think we'd still have a conflict of interest now that he has settled?"

"No, now that the lawsuit is over, go for it. But I've said it before, Mack, you and Bob should watch your back every minute as long as Archer is out there. He takes pleasure in killing people and would love to off you both."

"Yeah. We will. Gotta go and see Diego this afternoon. I'll let you know how things go."

Mack spoke through the prison intercom. "Diego, I never thought I would be in a position to ask for your help, but Archer seems to have gone underground. You know him from before in Colombia . . . any ideas?"

Diego shook his head slowly in disbelief. "You put him in the wind with your little legal games and now you come to me for help?" Diego laughed heartily, an indication his wounds were healing well. "I heard the suit that hired him took the pipe. That true?"

"Not exactly. We think Archer did him and took off with money, stock certificates, and a secret formula from the company."

"So now he has plenty of pesos for whatever he plans to do." Diego paused. "When you hunt for el tigre you must think like el tigre." He narrowed his eyes and clenched his jaw so hard, the muscles on each side of his face bulged.

"Okay. What?" Mack waited.

"Can he cash in the other stuff he took? When the cash is gone he will need more. He'll probably want to fence the stuff. Maybe you can pick up on him through that? But he's too slick for you. He'll hide in plain sight and always know his next moves. You'll always be playing catch-up, amigo. Sorry."

Mack slowly nodded, as if dawn was breaking in his head. "Diego, you may have figured it out. He'll be goin' to the marketplace. The dark marketplace."

Diego grinned slyly, "Claro, que si, Five-O. You're catching on. Maybe you're not as dumb as you look. I shouldn't help you. I want him for myself. But together, maybe we have a better chance, si?"

"More than a chance! You bet, amigo! Together, he's dealing with double trouble!"

Chapter *Thirty-Five*

Kevin Murray held a cup of coffee in both hands as he stood gazing through the large window of his mountain-top study. He felt a sudden chill thinking about where things might be heading, unconsciously pressing hard against the sides of the cup to feel its warmth.

"We know this man is ruthless, Mack. He's smart, has international connections, and will stop at nothing. He knows all the ins and outs. We really need to stay sharp to take him down."

Mack nodded solemnly in agreement. He knew Archer would be a huge challenge. "Diego and I were talking and we're thinking he's probably gone to the dark web. Whaddaya think, Kev?"

"Good bet. It's the quickest and easiest way to cash in the stolen cancer drug formula."

For a moment they stood watching through the glass as a strong gust of wind blew against the mountain sending the snow upwards past the window. Kevin said, "I never tire of watching this."

Kevin continued, "The trick would be to somehow suck him into a sting that could nail his ass. We would need someone he'd be willing to deal with. Someone on the inside."

"Someone like an international arms dealer?" Mack smirked knowingly.

"You remembered." Kevin thought a moment, looking very serious. "Yeah, that might work. Let me talk to our Israeli friend and get back to you."

Archer thought he heard something. *There it is again.* It wasn't loud, just a subtle brushing or rubbing noise. After a few seconds it came again, like a woodpecker tapping on the roof, but less persistent. More random. *I know that sound,* he thought. *Repetitive and determined. No, more like rushing. I know what it is. Men's sneakers hustling across concrete. Jesus, they've come for me!* Ted Archer tried to calm himself.

Gotta get to my MP-5 across the room. Too late. Ted Archer looked up from his bed into Diego's black eyes.

"Hola, Ted," he spat. *Diego, how did you get out of jail?*

"Adios, Ted." The gun pressed against his forehead exploded. *Strange. No pain. I'm sinking into a black hole. Faster and faster. Spinning. Spinning.*

Archer sprung from the pillow dripping sweat, his hands clutching the bed rails in a futile effort to stop the nightmarish spinning. Instinctively, he looked across the room to the MP-5. It was there. He jumped out of bed to check the small door downstairs. It was intact. But in that moment, emotionally spent, he kept turning the door knob over and over to reassure himself.

Splashing the last remnant of the nightmare away over the sink, he fretted, *C'mon, Ted. This isn't you. Shake it off.* It was dark—still a little early—but he stayed up anyway and fixed a coffee, denying the fear of returning to sleep and maybe back to that nightmare. *You'll be okay, Ted. Be calm. You need to act. Put the plan into motion; no second-guessing. Today is the day.* He suddenly spoke out loud, "You know me well, Diego. I always turn defense into offense. And today I am gonna be very offensive."

"How did you get them to give in, Mr. Reddy?" Maria was dumbfounded at the change of events. "Why would ABP want to settle so quickly? That's so much money!"

Avery shrugged. "Who knows what motivates people?" He had decided to not mention Mack's visit to Alfred Stewart. He rationalized, *No need for anyone to think there was coercion involved. After all, it was only right to let Stewart know about his vice-president, and he decided to do the right thing on his own. Anyway, if not completely ethical, it was the moral thing to do.* But Avery couldn't help chiding himself. *Being a lawyer means justifying anything to anybody at any time on any issue. For every rule there are a myriad of circumvents. Ah, well, it's a dirty job, but somebody's gotta do it.*

Mark and Julie were in shock over their share of the settlement. Mark said, "It won't bring back my brother, but at least our mom can get the medical treatment for her back now. That's one good thing that's come out of this disaster."

"And Mark and I got to know each other better." Julie blushed, hugging Mark's arm closer.

Avery asked, "Maria, where is Jose? I wanted for you all to come in today."

"Good question, Mr. Reddy. He said he would meet us here this morning. He'll be along soon." She peered through the window at the parking lot. *I sure hope so. He should be here by now.*

Chapter *Thirty-Six*

Archer parked across from the coffee shop next to Jose's Jeep. The kid left home the same time as his sister, but they went in different directions. Archer had to decide quickly: *Which one would be easier?* The question answered itself. As much as he would like to have gotten back at one of "*those broads*" for the humiliation he suffered back in the lab, the smart play was choosing the boy. *He looks the weaker of the two. If I take him, she'll go bonkers and Diego will see he'd better back off or I'll kill the kid.*

"Thanks, Mr. Butler. Great breakfast, as usual. See ya."

"Have a good day, Jose. Regards to Maria."

Jose crossed the street to the municipal parking lot and unlocked his driver's door. His next lucid thoughts came in throbbing waves. He was trussed up, blindfolded, gagged and bouncing around on carpeting in the rear of what he made out to be a van. He tried to yell. "Mmmm! Mmmmm!"

"Shut up, punk! Behave and maybe you'll come out of this all right." Archer threw a quick glance over his shoulder. He laughed and shouted, "Sodium pentothal wearing off yet, boy?" Jerking the wheel suddenly, he pitched the minivan back and forth. Jose rolled over, bumping against the van's wall. Disoriented and becoming nauseous, he panicked. *If I bring up breakfast, I could drown in my own vomit.* Refusing to give in to helplessness, Jose gritted his teeth and found the strength to hold back the terror building within. He scolded himself. *Toughen up! Be tough, Jose. Hang in until whatever comes next. If he wanted to kill me, I'd be dead by now.* The bouncing and disorientation continued, but Jose refused to let it rule him.

Archer made the drive from South Plainfield to Bayonne in under 45 minutes. Once Jose was secured in a small storage closet next to his upstairs office, he made the call.

Normally unfazed by much, Nezzie was spooked. She called Mack and in a panicky voice said. "Mack, I just got a call from Ted Archer. My caller ID shows it was from Jose Rodriguez' special phone. All Archer said was, 'I have Jose.

Tell Diego.'" Nezzie paused, composed herself and spoke slowly for emphasis, "Mack, Archer has grabbed Jose!"

Mack pulled off Route 22 into a Perkins Restaurant. "Archer's turning the tables. It's his style, Kidnapping. Nezzie, get Bob into the office ASAP and reach out to Maria." He hesitated a moment. "Don't tell her anything. Just tell her I need to see her right away. Meanwhile, I'll fill in Avery and stop to see Diego on my way in. I should be there in an hour."

Mack greeted Diego with a solemn expression. As Diego got closer to the glass, he grinned confidently. Picking up the intercom, his first words were, "Back for more help, Five-0?" But Diego's expression changed when he saw the look on Mack's face.

"We have a situation, Diego. Archer has Jose."

"What? Bastardo!" The veins in Diego's temples swelled. "I should've known. I told you he'd be one step ahead. What do you know?"

"We don't know anything yet. All we know is that Archer called saying he has Jose and to tell you. There's been no other contact."

Diego bit his lower lip and aimed a penetrating stare at Mack. "He is using you to communicate with me."

"Obviously."

"And what are you gonna do about it, Five-0?" Diego sat back and glared at Mack with cold, pained eyes.

"This is only an hour old, Diego. We're getting everyone together, but I thought you should know right away. It's kidnapping, so we have to bring in the police."

"No way. No cops." Diego shook his head. "This is personal, Five-0. He made it personal. It's him and me, now."

"Slow down, Diego. I didn't think you'd like it, but just hear me out. I have connections and ways to steer the case to the best guys. You and I have the same goal: to get Jose back and to take Archer down, right?"

"Yeah. But when you screw it up, my nephew gets hurt and I'll come looking for you."

"I can do this, Diego. We can't let Jose get caught in the middle. Just keep your friends on ice." Realizing the *ice* faux pas, Mack apologized, "I didn't mean ICE."

Diego glared back at the wise-guy remark, obviously angry and distressed. He sat back considering his position behind bars and hating that he wasn't out there taking care of Archer, himself, before something happened to Jose. He sighed, blinked a couple of times, softened his tone, and said, "I love that kid, Five O. He was my sister's youngest. The baby in the family. With us, it's all family. You better keep him safe. I'll give you twenty-four hours.

"Don't worry, Diego. We'll find him."

"Our choices are the feds, locals or state police, Mack." Bob Higgins sat on the edge of the conference room table. "The FBI is most experienced at handling kidnappings, but if we go to them, we'll be out in the cold. Not only that, the spirit of J. Edgar often reigns. You know: 'No glory? We don't play.'"

"Agreed."

"Since we don't know where he's holed up, we don't know which locals to go to. That leaves my old outfit, the New Jersey State Police."

"I think you're right, Bob. Why don't you give one of your buddies down there a heads up?" Mack grabbed his cell phone and headed for the door. "Nezzie, please call Kevin Murray and tell him I'm on the way over.

Twenty minutes later, Kevin met Mack at the door. He could see something serious had happened. "C'mon in. What's goin' on?"

"It's taken a big turn, Kevin. Now we have a kidnapping and the victim is none other than Jose Rodriguez, nephew of Diego Gomez, the Rahway prisoner I told you about. The one that tried to kill Archer."

"Oh yeah. The one Archer almost had killed, too."

"Right." They sat across from Kevin's desk close to his big window overlooking the valley below. "Kevin, those special phones you handed out a couple of weeks ago—did you by any chance include a GPS feature? The reason I ask is that Nezzie recognized the number that Archer called on as the one you assigned to Jose."

"I did. I kept the phone number assigned to each person and preloaded the phones with a covert GPS tracking app, just in case." Kevin winked. "Let's check it out."

Mack watched as a map came up on the computer screen. The data showed the phone was moving south along the New Jersey Turnpike.

"That's funny." Kevin frowned.

"What?"

"It shows the phone is traveling at 110 mph. Do you think Archer would risk being pulled over by a state trooper on the turnpike?"

Mack walked over to the window. "What a pair of balls! Kevin, think about it, what goes that fast on the turnpike?"

"Of course. Troopers." Kevin nodded his head with a half-smile. "He stuck the phone under the bumper of a trooper car. This guy is very clever, Mack. And bold. He's playing with us."

"Gomez is right. We're always doing catch-up with Archer. We've got to think of something to get up to speed and take his advantage away."

"What about that dark web angle? I made the call. My guy is up for playing a little gotcha game if you are."

"Mossad?" Mack asked, referring to Israeli national intelligence.

"Uh-huh. They keep a presence on the dark web. My friend and I discussed your case, and he thinks the secret drug formula has possibilities for a sting. His 'company' moves weapons and drugs around the globe. Not really, it's more like they make it look like they do. Really, they 'buy and sell' to other Mossad agents on the dark web posing as bad guys. They keep in touch with the criminal element this way and, in essence, become one with them. At least, it's a way you might be able to work Archer instead of him working you. It might be worth a try."

"It *is* worth a try, Kevin. Let's do it."

Chapter *Thirty-Seven*

"You gonna be smart and behave?"

Jose looked up at Archer, his back leaning against the wall. "What choice do I have?" Keeping himself together as best he could, Jose softly said, "At least I have a pot to piss in. Could ya please just loosen the handcuffs a little? I have no feeling in my fingers."

"You're a plucky kid. Not as weak as I expected. You cooperate and we'll get along fine." He adjusted the cuffs back a notch. Archer thought, *Hey, a small concession here and there encourages obedience.* "Now, you and I are gonna make a little video for your uncle just to show him you're okay. You *will* do and say exactly what I say or painful cuffs will be the least of your problems. Comprende?

"You don't know my uncle. I'm not so sure he cares that much about me. If he had the chance, he'd probably use me for bait to get at you." Jose looked at the floor. "I hope I'm wrong."

"So do I, kid. So do I."

Avraham—or Avi, as his friends called him—was hunched over his laptop in the back room of a small café in Efrat, a small town 18 kilometers south of Jerusalem. Avi was in his late-60's but appeared much older. The long white hair on either side of his otherwise bald head gave him a Ben Gurion look. Now retired, his past life as a Mossad agent had taken him around the world placing him in too many stressful circumstances which collectively had exacted a heavy physical and emotional toll. Avi walked with a limp and had only limited use of his left arm. He often joked, "This is what happens to you in combat when you confuse your zigs from your zags." But, all in all, Avi felt life was good. He enjoyed his retirement, especially his grandchildren. Retired? Then again, no one really retires from the Mossad.

The younger agent teased Avi, keenly aware of his elder's frustration with all-things-computer. "So, tell me bubala, what's got your shorts all twisted up today?"

"This internet thing has me confused. Dark web, dark schweb! In the old days we did things in a more, shall we say, direct fashion. Be a mensch and help me out here, Samuel."

His annoyance apparent, Avi turned from the lap top and said, "My friend in the states has a big problem. Murder, big-time theft, and kidnapping. I was hoping we could help him out." Avi went on to recount his conversation with Kevin Murray.

"So, if I get this right, you want to put some bait out there that would be of interest to this Archer person."

"Right, but we have to schlep carefully. This guy is a trained intelligence officer himself, though now working the other side. A little reverse psychology might be just what we need." Avi smiled at his young protégé. "I'll supply the shovel. You do the digging, as only you can."

Samuel, forever respectful of the older man's wisdom and his penchant for enigmatic commentary, grinned and eagerly traded places with Avi at the laptop.

"Let's see. The best way to root around in the dark web is with the Tor browser. Here we go."

Their phishing expedition began.

Mack and Bob reviewed the short video for the fourth time. It started out with a zoom to the front page of the *New York Times*, purposefully showing the date. Then it zoomed back and to the right where Jose was seated against the wall, handcuffed to a metal radiator.

A voice in the background, obviously Archer's, said, "Go ahead, Jose."

Reading from a paper held out from behind the video camera, Jose spoke. "Uncle, I am not hurt. So far, Mr. Archer has fed me and allowed me to use the bathroom. But he will not let me go until you set it up so he can get away. He will give you further instructions later." Jose looked up at his captor for approval, then pleadingly back at the camera. The video went to gray.

"Whaddaya think, Bob?"

Bob thought a moment, then said, "Jose looks pretty miserable, but I don't get the impression Archer has physically abused him. Yet."

"Yeah. No bruises or blood. But we know Archer. Push comes to shove, he would kill Jose without a second thought." Mack swiveled his chair around, got up and stretched. He asked, "Anything stand out in the video that would help us? I mean the background stuff."

Bob tugged his right ear, deep in thought. "The radiator suggests an old building. The wall behind him hasn't been painted in decades. And did you see when the newspaper moved up? The narrow-style hardwood flooring along the edge of the screen was really grungy."

"So, he's holed up in a run-down place, but he has to have running water and electricity. How many of those places are there?"

Bob nodded in agreement. "Jose did say there was a bathroom."

"He's renting an old apartment or something like it, and I would put it in a city area where you'd find those kinds of buildings."

"Mack, play it once more. Close your eyes and listen this time. Let's try to identify any background noises."

They turned up the volume so loud Nezzie came into the conference room, her curiosity piqued. "What's goin' on? I can't even think out there."

Chapter Thirty-Seven

Mack shushed her and pointed to a side chair. They played it again.

Nezzie looked from Mack to Bob and back again. "Don't you two hear it? It's right at the end after the boy says, 'He will give you further instructions later.' It's like a horn or something."

Mack played it again and agreed. "I didn't hear it before, but I do now. It's a strange low moaning sound, like a fog horn."

Bob sat up straight and exclaimed, "They're near the water. That was the sound of a ship's air horn. It starts out weak and grows, as the air pushes through. Gotta be near water, a river. A big river, I think."

Mack said, "Put all of what we know together, and it looks like he's on a waterfront."

"Yeah, maybe an old warehouse. But where? The Hudson? Or Delaware?"

Maria arrived. Nezzie ushered her into the conference room. Mack, uncomfortable with what he was about to say, motioned Maria into a chair.

"Maria, we've got some troubling news. There's no easy way to say this. Jose has been taken by Ted Archer." Mack followed that up, speaking quickly in a higher octave, "But we pretty much know Jose's okay at this point, because Archer sent over a video."

Maria gasped, her face scrunching and tears forming. "Oh my God! First mama, now Jose." She hugged herself and cried hard as Mack awkwardly placed his hand on her shoulder. After several minutes she took a breath and asked, "Can I see the video?"

"Go ahead, Bob." All remained silent while the video played again.

Chapter *Thirty-Eight*

Bob Higgins parked in the visitor's parking lot at New Jersey State Police headquarters in West Trenton. A seven-story, shiny new building replaced a hodgepodge assembly of temporary trailers formerly housing various investigative units.

Traditionally, a strong sense of camaraderie exists among Jersey's state troopers, both active duty and retired. So, when Bob identified himself, he was greeted warmly and ushered into the NJSP Intelligence Unit where he met with his old friend, Major George Hawkins.

"Hey, Bob. Long time no see."

Bob replied, "The last time I saw you, you were wearing your new sergeant's stripes."

"Yeah. About 10 years ago. What's up? I hear you are a private eye now."

Bob took a seat and cut to the chase. He told Hawkins about ABP, Archer, the Lott murder, McGinn's death, the kidnapping and all that he and Mack were up against.

"Whew! That's a lot. You've been busy. So, the locals aren't cooperating, Bob?"

"Nah. We're a little stymied: The local police and prosecutor aren't convinced Henry Lott died from anything but an unfortunate accident. 'Speeding and loss of control,' they said. The Basking Ridge PD sees McGinn's death as a suicide, but we know better. Then there's our drug dealer in East Jersey State Prison complicating everything by sending MS-13 out to get Archer. Archer bumps off one of his attackers, then kidnaps the dirt bag's nephew, Jose. So Archer's in the wind with Jose, ABP's company stock certificates, and a secret pharmaceutical formula. We need some official help."

"Tell ya what. I'll set up a case and assign one of my crew to look into this. From what you're telling me, you're pretty much down the road in terms of investigation. I'll have our investigator check in with you guys right away, okay?"

"Couldn't be better, George. I mean, Major." Bob teased Hawkins with a brisk salute.

"Cut the bullshit, Bob, and get outta here."

Avi sipped his mint tea. "The first thing we do, Samuel my boy, is to pose as a Russian oligarch. You know, those guys are always into something crooked. They would steal your grandma's panties, if there was a ruble in it." Avi stopped the lesson for a moment and quipped, "By the way, how is your grandma?" He winked and flirtatiously raised his eyebrows twice.

Samuel shook his head in mock disgust.

Avi continued, "Instead of looking to buy a secret formula, we will offer one for sale on the dark web. The oligarchs specialize in stealing state secrets, so why not a drug formula? Reverse psychology, my boy. Get it?"

Samuel didn't get it. "Why would Archer be interested in that? He's selling, not buying."

"Look, this gonif needs a connection. If he sees someone else selling something similar to what he has, he will want to see how they do it. He'll be asking, 'Who are the buyers?

Maybe I can get in on this.' I'm hoping he makes contact looking to either rip us off by grabbing our buyer or, better yet, joining with us to sell two secret formulas. Either way, we make contact. See?"

"I get it. We are both the buyer and the seller, waiting for him to find us. When he does, we schmooze with him. We give him the spiel and, hopefully, the schmuck bites."

"Schmart kid."

"And if *he's* smart, he'll have an account in the Caymans and look to turn the goods over once he gets confirmation of a deposit, no?"

"Ah, there's the tricky part, my boy. He won't trust us and we won't trust him. So, what's left?" Avi stood with his eyes looking skyward, hands out, palms up, shrugging his shoulders.

Samuel slowly nodded his head. "A meet."

Avi bopped his young protégé's head and said, "This round hairy thing is working, after all. Let's get to work."

With his right hand cuffed to a radiator, sleeping on the hard floor left Jose tired and stiff. He tried to keep track of Archer's movements, even when out of sight. The sound of a drill buzzing and light tapping from time to time came from beyond the confines of the second-floor office. Jose thought, *he's building something.*

Jose was right. Archer was putting the finishing touches on what he called his early-warning system. He had two drones stationed at opposing corners on the roof and cameras pointed up and down the narrow roadway, as well as toward the building's back side. All close approaches were covered. What he needed now was a long-range camera to capture the nearest intersection where a raiding party would most likely stage before rushing in on him.

Hooking what he would need to his belt, Archer carefully climbed the rickety ladder to the upper roof and looked around. *There it is. Let's see, the range-finder shows 942 feet due west. I'll line up this last camera just so and go down and confirm I have all bases covered.*

Back in the second-floor office, he checked his monitors. *All working. Good.* Archer settled into the swivel chair at the old wooden desk and started pecking away on the computer. He opened Bing and typed in a web address. He monitored the internet traffic at certain IP addresses he thought might be productive. He rooted around on the dark web for two hours before finding one that had promise.

Hmm. This guy's trying to peddle a new cancer formula. If he's looking to sell it on this site, it's probably hijacked from some company. Let's try the private email he lists.

Ted Archer—like a fish taking the bait—was about to be phished, himself.

Chapter *Thirty-Nine*

Nezzie poked her head into Mack's office and announced, "State Police Detective Wilson to see ya, Mack." As she pulled back from the doorway, she batted her eyes and smirked.

"Good morning, Mr. Mackey. I'm Detective Cheryl Wilson. Major Hawkins sent me up to meet with you and Bob Higgins." She looked around Mack's office. "Is he here, too?"

"Uh, no. Bob won't be here until lunchtime." Somewhat taken aback, Mack stood and awkwardly offered her a chair.

"Here's my card. From what I was told, this is more than a kidnapping case, but that's the most pressing item, right?" She was all business. Dressed in a dark blue pant suit, Detective Wilson could have passed for a company employee in the nearby corporate office complex. In her early 30's, she was a trim, purposeful brunette and totally self-assured.

Mack, yet to regain his composure, stammered, "We, uh, we appreciate you being here, detective."

"Wouldn't it be easier to call me, Cheryl? And I understand everyone calls you Mack."

"Sure. That works." Mack called out for Nezzie. "Would you please get with Bob, Nezzie, and tell him Detective Wilson is here." He winked at Cheryl and said, "No need to give him all the details, okay?"

Cheryl, with a patient expression, looked down at her folded hands and said, "Okay, I'm not what you expected. I get that. Female detectives, especially in the state police, are still considered an oddity but we've been in uniform for several decades now. So why not in plainclothes, too? Believe me, Mack, there are times when it's a big advantage."

"Look, Cheryl, I didn't mean to come across, uh, wrong. You're a state trooper detective and that's good enough for me." Trying to smooth over his first response, Mack added, "And you're right. I admit I had an initial surprised reaction but that's over now. Some of us dinosaurs can't help our upbringing, so don't hold that against us. We *are* adjusting with the times. Now, can we get down to business?"

Cheryl smiled, appreciating Mack's straight forward openness. "Sure. Where do you want to start?" She took out a note pad and shifted in her chair, signaling a "getting down to business" attitude.

Mack started with Henry Lott's death and laid out all the subsequent events. He identified all of the people involved, along with his impressions of them. He also provided her with a copy of Bob's field notes. It took nearly two hours to bring Cheryl up to date.

"Well, we still don't have real evidence that Archer used a novel electronic device to kill Henry Lott, do we?" Detective Wilson was quick on the uptake.

"No. We're working on that. We're thinking an onboard computer examination could yield evidence of tampering. That's in the works. In the meantime, we're trying to find Archer and get Jose back, as well as what Archer took from ABP."

"And that's the reason I'm here. Major Hawkins told me to provide whatever help I can—particularly in terms of official standing—to find Archer and Jose."

Bob Higgins arrived. He never flinched when introduced to Cheryl, noting Mack's smug expression at the time. "You'll have to excuse Mack, Cheryl. He's a leftover fossil from way back. Besides, Hawkins already filled me in about you before I left HQ yesterday. Mack, I'll have you know this detective—and without any backup—took down a bank robber last year. She's one tough trooper and we're lucky to have her on this case."

Cheryl blushed. "Thanks, Bob. Let's hope we can add to your investigation and bring this guy down, too."

Diego Gomez was an impatient man with too much time on his hands to just sit and think. He had to do something to help get Jose back. He and his younger companion walked around the prison yard.

"Whitey, I've been watching you. You're smarter than most of the idiots in here. I need your help. This is very important to me, and I will see you get paid very well. In three days, you'll be out on the street." He came to a halt and took the younger man's elbow, steering him away from a group forming nearby

"Normally, I would use my MS-13 boys, but they didn't do too good for me last time. Besides, as an Anglo, you won't be connected to me."

"Whatever you need, brother, you got it."

Despite Diego's assessment, Roger "Whitey" Whitman was a three-time loser with no desire to reform his life. He knew he'd be back in the slammer eventually. His goal was to see how long he could stay street-side. As it happened,

Diego's request turned out to be perfect timing. He was broke. He would jump parole, he knew that, but money would be his biggest challenge. Whatever Diego proposed had to be far better than knocking over convenient stores again—and with a bigger paycheck.

Diego went into detail. "What I need you to do is to keep track of a private eye and let him lead us to Jose and to that guy that I was telling you about who has my nephew, Jose. You'll need to get some helpers, so make good choices. I'm going to give you a number in Colombia and a code you'll need to get your payment. You'll get 10 large now to get set up and another 15 when you have Jose safely in your hands."

"I will not let you down, jefe."

Diego made a sour face. "Don't push your artificial Spanish on me, Whitey. It don't work. Just stay glued to that P.I. and find my nephew. The P.I.'s name is Mack Mackey and his office is along Route 22 in Greenbrook. Here, I wrote it down for you." Before turning and walking away, he drilled his piercing dark eyes into Whitey's and said, "Do this and do it right. You do not want me hunting you down and punishing you if you fail. Let's put it this way: You will not die peacefully in your sleep."

Whitey blinked. "I understand, boss."

Avi was upbeat. "Samuel, we have a bite. Take a look at this private email we just got. It looks like our trap might be working."

Over Avi's shoulder Samuel read aloud. "He says, 'Interested in your product. I have one too. Any chance we could team up?'" Samuel mused, "'Team up.' That's an American colloquialism, yes?"

"College boy, stop using big words. Yeah, he talks like an American. It's him! When did it come in?"

Samuel checked the email's heading. "That clinches it. It came in this morning at 1:08 a.m. our time, which would make it 6:08 p.m. in New York. It's him. It's Archer." Samuel stood upright and asked, "Now what? Our fish is nibbling, Avi. How do we sink the hook and reel him in?"

Avi leaned back and lit his pipe. "We wait, my boy. We give the fish some time to nibble some more. Have a bagel. Cream cheese?"

Chapter *Forty*

For the first time in his life, Whitey was rolling in dough. The $10,000 wire transfer actually came through from Diego's South American contact. He kept $3,000 in his pocket and hid $7,000 under a raised floor board beneath the kitchen sink. The small Irvington apartment he rented wasn't much, but it beat the hell out of his former accommodations in tier nine at Rahway prison.

An hour later, Roger "Whitey" Whitman was sitting in the back of Hal's Candy Shop on Broad Street, two blocks from the Prudential Center in downtown Newark. He was elated. "I can't believe it, Hal. One day I'm trying to survive in the can and each day I asked myself, 'Will I be alive tomorrow?' The next thing I know I'm on the street flush with coin. Unbelievable!"

Hal Benson, an ex-con himself, ran the candy shop. It was more a front for whatever illegal activities came along. Hal, the quintessential entrepreneur, was into gambling, drugs, stolen property, and con jobs. He and Whitey had "served together" in various prisons in the tri-state area, so it was to be expected when Whitey achieved his latest liberty that he would celebrate with Hal.

"So, here we are again, Whitey," Hal remarked. "Both on the bricks at the same time, and you with full pockets. Fuckin' amazing!"

Whitey exhaled rich smoke from one of Hal's Cuban cigars retrieved from under the front counter. "Yeah, but we got a tricky job to do, pal. It ain't gonna be easy, and ain't no way I can avoid it or do it alone." Whitey's attitude suddenly changed from elated to somber.

"Diego Gomez. You remember him, the Colombian who had Jack sliced up. Well, his nephew was grabbed by this dirty DEA guy." He sucked deeply on the cigar and coughed. "Anyway, we gotta follow a P.I. to find where the dirt bag has Diego's nephew and get him back, somehow."

Hal pointed out the obvious. "Hey, slow down. Diego's off the street. You got his green, so why not sit back and live a little? You don't owe him nothin'."

"Wrong. Diego would have me cut up before we paid our first bar bill." Neither one said a thing as the words hung in the air.

Whitey looked up from the worn sofa with his head cocked inquisitively to one side. "You ever kill anybody, Hal?"

"No, but—"

"Neither did I." He gave a half-laugh and said, "The closest I ever came was when I shot the hell out of that ATM next to the Starbucks in Kearny. Remember?" Whitey and Hal enjoyed a moment of amused recollection, but Whitey's next comment brought them back to reality.

"Gomez lost count of his victims a long time ago. We don't want to be on his shit list, do we?" Whitey blew an ash off the hot end of the cigar. "No, I ain't about to mess with the dude. So, I need you to put a crew together for me. I need four good guys. We take care of this and I'll take care of you really well with what I'll have comin' to me. And for now, I'm outta here. I gotta go and buy some stuff while you make some calls."

At DICK's Sporting Goods on Route 22 in Union, New Jersey, Whitey pushed the cart up and down the aisles. *Let's see: multi-channel two-way radios, good long-range binoculars, and a porta potty.* He also picked up a new casual wardrobe for himself. He thought, *Hey, Gomez, I may be working for you, but as long as I am, you're gonna feed me and put some threads on my back.* At a local Walmart he bought heavy-duty wire cutters, a screw-driver set, small and large crowbars and a 12-pound sledge hammer. He was almost outfitted for the job.

Back at Hal's shop, Whitey brought up a sensitive subject. "I picked up a lot of stuff this afternoon, but we're gonna need protection, Hal. Know the right guy for some weapons?"

Hal peered back over his shoulder from stocking shelves behind the counter. The shop was empty. "Uh, I guess so," he said, nervously. He didn't make eye contact.

Whitey understood Hal's reluctance. "Hey, I know you never carried a piece on a job. It kept your slammer-time shorter. If you don't want in on this, okay. But I need your connections, pal. Can do?"

"Don't get me wrong, Whitey. I'll help you where I can, but," Hal emphasized, "I *don't* do guns. And I can't do the job with ya."

"Understood. But I need some good help. The guy we're after is an ex-SEAL and DEA agent. And, from what I'm told, a bad-ass nasty one, so . . ."

"I can fix you up." Hal's face relaxed, relieved that Whitey wasn't drawing him in. "I made some calls and pulled a crew together. We can meet here at around 10:00 tonight. That okay with you?"

"Do I know any of them?"

"Nah. All young ones, but tough. Two were special forces and got in jams, something about selling military stuff on the black market. Good soldiers, though. The third one is smart. A little mouthy, but smart. They all have rap sheets and are willing to work. You'll be happy. And they'll be very happy for a payday."

"So, that's four including me. I need one more."

"I'll think about it. Maybe one of them knows somebody."

That night Whitey met with his crew. The two ex-special forces soldiers didn't say much but Whitey liked them right away. They would follow orders. The third—the one Hal called smart—was another matter. He had a swaggering way about him and talked too much

His name was Phillip Ogden—and because he was from Philadelphia, his nickname, naturally, was Philly. He'd done three years for beating a fellow karate student to death in Camden when the other guy made eyes at Philly's girl.

"'Manslaughter,' they said. My lawyer got me a lower charge, saying it was just play-fighting in karate class. An accident." Philly looked around the room and laughed. "Play-fighting. Like, I didn't mean to drive his nose bone into his brain. Got lucky on that one."

The two ex-special forces soldiers locked eyes, knowingly. *Some tough guy, all mouth!*

Whitey also saw through Philly. *Arrogant wise guy, too much attitude*. Whitey told him so. "Philly, if you come on this job, you'll knock off the bullshit. Hal tells me you're smart but I don't need a smart *ass*. Dial it back or get out. Got it? You're working with experienced people here, make sure some of it rubs off."

"Hey, whatever, man. I need the scratch. I'm in. I'm in."

Whitey glanced over at the two spec-soldiers. One was smiling at the way Whitey yanked the kid's chain, the other nodded ever-so- slightly. Whitey nodded back. *They'll keep him in line.*

The next day Hal completed his crew. Detective Ed Rutkowski was fired from the Newark Police Department when a stack of hundred-dollar bills was found on him after a drug raid. He was about to move it out of his precinct locker when a lieutenant happened to turn the corner and spot Ed jamming the stack into his gym bag. It all went downhill from there.

Ed had hung tough and wouldn't answer questions. While it seemed obvious where the money had come from, it couldn't be proven, so he was fired and not arrested. The money? Well, that disappeared into thin air, somewhere between the lieutenant and a captain. Or was it between the captain and the chief of the narcotics squad? Who knew? Who cared? Bottom line: Ed was a goner, and he was bitter.

Whitey had his crew. "All I ask is that you all do what I say. We can't make mistakes with this guy." He looked around the small back room. *Two ex-special forces, a gutsy kid, and an ex- cop. Not bad.*

Whitey laid out all the equipment, including weapons: five handguns, a sawed-off 12-gauge double-barreled shotgun. Lastly, and most admired by the two spec-soldiers, an M40A3 U.S. Marine sniper rifle with a scope attached. All were stolen and came with ample ammo.

"Now, here's the plan." Whitey laid it out.

Chapter *Forty-One*

ezzie hollered, "It's Kevin Murray, Mack. Pick up on one."

"What's up, Kevin. Anything from your friend?"

"Yeah. Avi thinks he's got Archer interested and on hold"

"Outstanding!"

"Avi is posing as a Russian oligarch with a stolen British drug formula for sale. How's that for bait! Like we were hoping, Archer went searching through the dark web to find a buyer for the cancer drug formula he took off McGinn. He went for it when he saw someone else was trying to sell one, too."

"Pow, Kevin!"

"Yeah. Archer wants to team up with 'our Russians' and deal with their supposed buyer to cash in with the ABP formula. Avi is sitting there as seller and buyer. Very clever. At this point, Avi has put a price for the formula around 20 million U.S. That should be enough to hook Archer in. Avi's reverse-psychology play is nothing short of genius. They're doing a great job of working him up, Mack."

"Oh yeah. This is great. But how is Avi gonna draw Archer out?"

"He's working on that. He plans to hold out until Archer agrees to a meet. He already told Archer in the second round of emails he doesn't trust him and wants something to prove that Archer actually has something of value—and that he isn't law enforcement. That would be normal for these guys."

"Sounds good. And here's more good news at our end. The state police are in on it now. This could go down fast, Kevin, and time is important, so pass it along as soon as you get something from Avi. We can move on a moment's notice."

With all the excitement swirling around, Kevin had become intrigued. "You got it, Mack. Just one other thing. You know—with this electronic-savvy guy, Archer—you might need an old techie working with you in the field. Got any room for me?"

"You bet, pal. I thought you wouldn't be able to resist. You're in."

Samuel called Avi. "Another email just came in from Archer. You should come down here right away."

When Avi arrived, the first thing he said was, "This better be good, my boy, I was just about to make love to Deborah Kerr when your phone call woke me up at the worse possible moment.

Samuel smiled good-naturedly, "Your dream girl can wait until you get back, Avi. I think you'll be happy with this.

"No, she won't be there when I get back. She never is." He grabbed at his glasses dangling on his chest and impatiently pushed them on. "Let's see what you have."

Avi quickly read through the email and said, "Happy? I'm more than happy. I'm delighted. "The schmuck is going for it. Send back that we need to have our own bio-scientist take a look at what he has before we agree to anything. Tell him our expert needs to inspect only one page of the formula to know if it's real or not. Tell him we understand he wouldn't part with it without full payment, so let's meet and inspect each other's documents before we go forward. He could bring his own expert."

"Won't he be suspicious about a meet?"

"Sure, to be expected on both sides. He will suggest a safe place for him that we won't like. We will do the same and he will reject our choice. It will go back and forth for a while until we both agree on a neutral spot. That's the way it is and has always been, my boy."

"Hmm." Samuel rubbed his chin in deep thought.

"What?"

"If we finally get him to show up, we'll need a team to follow him after the meet, right?" Samuel went on thoughtfully, "Hopefully, it will lead back to wherever he's holding the kidnapped boy. This is a lot to pull off, Avi."

"Yup, but our guys know what they're doing at the other end. We just need to do our part well."

Archer pulled his old Navy sea bag out of the back of the van and stored it in a second rental space along the river about a half-mile north of his new man cave. This was just a small one-car garage, but it suited his purpose perfectly. As he jogged back toward the warehouse, Archer, the ex-Navy SEAL, recalled what an old chief petty officer once told him, *Always a Plan B, Ted. Always a Plan B. Never be caught without an escape hatch.*

He woke Jose with a kick to the leg. "I'm moving you into the bathroom. You'll be able to move around more while I'm gone."

"You're going?" Sitting up stiffly, Jose squinted through his cobwebs.

Archer led Jose into the bathroom and, instead of the short-leashed handcuff setup, he attached a chain to a metal ring he'd screwed tightly into the floor, making the final turns with a metal bar. He clicked the handcuff to the chain.

"You'll be able to reach the throne this way. I'll be gone about eight hours, if all goes well. Here's some 7-Eleven sandwiches and water. Make it last."

"Thanks."

"It ain't a favor. I just don't want you to stink by the time I get back.

As Archer descended the metal steps, his systematic and ingrained thought process was whirling forward. *First London, then Barcelona, then Athens, of all places. They're nuts if they think I'm going anywhere I don't have good cover. Dumbass Russians. If I say New York, it's gonna be New York. Gotta let them know who's boss.*

Avi chuckled, "The putz. He wants New York? He can have New York. We knew he wouldn't stray far from his base. That's the thing about good tradecraft. It's predictable, but only to someone with better tradecraft. And that's me." Avi joyfully danced the *Kuma Eha* until his arthritis got the better of him.

Samuel dialed the secure number at the Israeli mission to the United Nations and handed the phone to Avi. "It's Yuri Postny, your 'Russian' friend."

Avi eagerly grabbed the phone and shouted, "Shalom, my brother. Do you miss the desert?"

"What desert? It's almost gone, thanks to the developers. What's on your devious mind, Avi? You don't call me here in the center of the universe with small talk."

"How would you like to be Russian for a day?"

"As a Russian Jew, I have a choice?"

Avi chuckled, "I know. I know." He filled Yuri in on the case and, since he was part of the Israeli delegation to the

United Nations, Yuri happened to be in the right place for the job. And his Mossad credentials made him the perfect choice.

"For you, I will do it. But only because you saved my ass on the outskirts of Beirut in the '82 war. I haven't forgotten. I owe you, my friend. So, how do we go about it?"

"I will get back to you. We have to coordinate with my New Jersey contact."

"Do I get to wear my Cossack hat?"

"Same old schmuck. No over-acting, please."

Chapter *Forty-Two*

Mack's small conference room had never been this crowded. Mack and Nezzie, Bob Higgins, State Police Detective Cheryl Wilson and her boss, Major Hawkins, and Kevin Murray were all trying to pack in tightly around the table.

Bob said, "Mack, I hate to complain, but this reminds me of Avery's mini-conference room. Do you think if this goes down the right way you could maybe get a bigger office? We're professionals, not sardines."

Mack wise-cracked back, "It's all part of forming a tight-ly-knit team, Bob."

Once the coffee and donuts were passed around, Mack began. "To recap, we have the kidnapping of a drug king-pin's nephew by ex-SEAL and disgraced DEA agent, Ted Archer, who incidentally has murdered several people recently."

Mack paused and looked around the room. "I don't need to say, he's a very dangerous guy and we need to keep that in mind. We believe he has in his possession company stock certificates and a secret cancer drug formula, which a now-deceased vice president of ABP stole from the company safe. Our job is to find Archer and get to the nephew, Jose Rodriguez. We need to get the kid back safely, as well as the stolen items, if possible. Any questions or comments before we go further?"

Kevin Murray spoke first. "I have some more info. My Israeli friends have set up a sting, and it is apparently bearing fruit. Archer wants to sell the cancer drug formula and has—or so he thinks—joined with Russian criminals to do so. A meet has been scheduled in New York at the United Nations cafeteria. At that time, Archer is to show good faith by producing one page of the formula for inspection by our 'Russians.' This creates an opportunity to tail Archer back to wherever he is holding Jose. Major Hawkins, I believe you have something to add?"

"Yes. Based on data provided by Mack and Bob, as well as their affidavits, we went to a judge and obtained a court order to attach a GPS device on any automobile Archer would be driving. I have also been authorized by Colonel Miller to call upon the full resources of the state police whenever we need it.

Bob observed, "The United Nations building. Wow! That will be a surveillance nightmare. We're gonna need all the help we can get."

"It will be difficult, but it's our only option right now," Mack said.

The meeting continued.

Parked a quarter mile west of Mack's office, Whitey sat behind the wheel of a rented Dodge van with his passenger, former Newark detective Ed Rutkowski. Philly was posted across from the office in the parking lot of a pizza shop. The Motorola radios had simplex channels—unable to send signals through a repeater—so the range was limited to line of sight, three or four miles at most.

Whitey lifted the radio, adjusted its squelch knob and said, "Philly, anything yet?"

"Nope. Same cars in the lot. The vans and two unmarked detective four-doors."

The ex-special forces team was waiting in another van a mile east on Route 22. It was doubtful their target would have a reason to go westerly. All bases were covered.

Whitey instructed, "They have to come this way when they leave. I will decide which one to tail. I can see the turn-around from here, so when one of them heads east, I will let you all know."

Double-clicks.

Nezzie refilled the coffee cups.

Detective Cheryl Wilson said, "Bob's right, Mack. There are so many ways to get into and out of that building, to say nothing of New York City itself. He could get lost in the crowd easily. Ever try to do a surveillance in the city?"

"Actually, we have. It's tough. We'll have to try and outguess him. First, what means of transportation will he use? Will he drive in? Take a bus? A train? The ferry?" Mack looked around the table, encouraging discussion.

Bob Higgins speculated, "I can't see him without wheels. Buses and trains will box him in without evasion prospects. No, he will use a car or van, but he'll be looking for a tail, for sure."

Kevin's cell phone vibrated. He looked back up at the group. "It's my Israeli pal, Avi." He stepped out to take the call.

Chapter Forty-Two

Major Hawkins was explaining the method used to acti-
vate his SWAT team when Kevin came back in. "Avi says
the meeting is set for 7 p.m. this Friday in the cafeteria." His
expression became clouded. "It will be dark by then."

"Well, that being the case, he'll have just as hard a time
spotting us as we will him," Mack said sarcastically. "It will
be a level playing field. Let's meet here at 1p.m. on Friday.
We'll play it by ear, if we have to. We have no choice." He
turned to Bob and said, "Can you go into the city now and
reconnoiter around the UN?"

"I'm on it." Bob left and, after negotiating the turn-
around, drove his mini-van east on Route 22 with Philly and
the ex-special forces team on his tail. Whitey and Rutkowski
played catch-up. Together, they triple-teamed Bob Higgins all
the way to New York.

Archer did his own reconnoiter. He left his mini-van in
the UN parking garage and had an early lunch in the cafeteria. He studied everything: the food-service employees, the
foot-traffic flow, the locations of exits and the security guard
standing off to one side. He had no intention of coming in here

cold on Friday night. After lunch, he walked around, fitting in with the tourists. Once outside, he—along with dozens of sightseers—passed a large sculpture of a revolver, its barrel tied in a knot. He laughed out loud, thinking, *if they wanted a peace symbol, it should've been a politician with his head tied in a knot."*

At that same instant, Bob Higgins approached from the opposite direction. He was surrounded by scores of visitors on their way into the west entrance. The first thing he saw was the large gun barrel tied in a knot. He smiled to himself, thinking, *so this is where the anti-gun lobby started.*

Keeping Bob in view, Philly pulled to the curb, lifted his radio and shouted excitedly, "Whitey, dude's goin' in the west entrance to the freakin' UN building. Whaddya want me to do?"

"Get out and follow him in. Leave it running; we'll get your van. Don't lose him!"

Archer stepped aside as the sprinting young man brushed against him and disappeared into the west entrance. *New Yorkers, always in a goddamn hurry.*

Three floors up, Yuri Postny rotated in his office chair. Cradling his phone between his head and neck, he parted the blinds and stared down at the west entrance. His view was limited to the usual crowd of visitors swirling past the revolver with the twisted barrel. As he waited for his call to Avi to go through, his gaze was fixed on the unique sculpture. He thought, *I wonder how many people know that "The Knotted Gun" was inspired by the shooting death of John Lennon.*

Samuel answered and turned the call over to Avi. Yuri couldn't help smiling at Avi's string of nervous comments about operating the sting. *There he goes again. Fretting over details. It's 1982 all over again!*

"Avi, don't worry. Relax. Breathe. We have a plan. The Jersey state cops are in on it, too. You have done all you could. You've done good." Unable to resist a jab between friends, he said, "Leave it to the *professionals*, from here on, my friend."

"Putz!" Avi grinned. "Go screw yourself."

Whitey and Rutkowski retrieved Philly's van. "What's he doin' now, Philly?"

"He's looking around in the cafeteria. He just sat down. He's on his cell and watching everybody. Maybe he's waiting for somebody. I can't tell."

An hour later Philly followed Bob to his van and watched him drive away. "I don't know what he was up to. It looked like maybe he was casing the joint. He didn't meet or talk to anyone."

Whitey gathered his crew together in a nearby parking lot. "Let's think about this. He leaves the meeting in Jersey and drives straight here. He makes phone calls while looking all around, like, checking things out. Then he leaves." Whitey shrugged and searched the faces of his crew.

Philly, the supposed smart one, sat there clueless. One of the ex-specs remarked, "It looks to me like he was doing recon work. Like settin' something up."

Ed Rutkowski, the banished cop, smirked. He had it figured it out. "They're running a sting on Archer. He's gonna show up here and that guy was scoping it out for the meet."

Whitey narrowed his eyes and slowly nodded his head. "Jesus. You're good. That's gotta be it. Okay, from now on we switch to watching what goes on in that cafeteria. Philly, see what you can do about getting us a room nearby. We'll set up rotating shifts until we know what's happening." He finished

258

with a warning. "Remember, when we spot Archer, we have to follow him to where he's keeping the kid. Then we have to figure out how to get the kid out alive. If Archer gets in the way, too bad for him."

Whitey bought a map of New York City.

Chapter *Forty-Three*

Mack was under fire—that is, from Penny and Maria. But he was holding his ground.

"Absolutely not! You are not trained. If you come along, the others will be distracted and worried about protecting you." Mack was adamant. They would not be going along on the New York surveillance job.

Penny was just as unyielding. "Why not? Just because we're not muscle-bound macho men? What century are you in?"

Maria argued, "Oh, c'mon, Mack, this is no time to be a chauvinist. Think about it. What if you need immediate medical attention for one of the guys? We're trained nurses. Penny sees that kind of stuff every day in the ER. Hey, blood and guts are no stranger to me, either." She looked back at Penny for support.

"Right. We don't need to carry guns. Just let us bring our emergency kits along and stay back unless we're needed. It would be good to have immediate medical attention instead of waiting for EMTs that could take up to half an hour." She stopped and with an apologetic look to Maria added, "And we really don't know what kind of shape Jose will be in when we find him." In unison, both Penny and Maria cried, "Please!"

Outnumbered—and out-argued—Mack relented. "Okay, but you ride with Kevin Murray and his electronic gear. He'll stay on the Jersey side of the river and will be called in if and only if we need him." He shook his head and grumbled, "I know when I'm beat."

Mack's reticence had nothing to do with gender. It was that lingering sense of loss from five years before when his Margie lay dying, her body wracked with cancer, and the helplessness he felt unable to do anything about it. It was fear of losing someone close again. He caught Penny's eye. She smiled softly, privately, knowingly. Her unhurried blink said, "I understand."

A faint, tentative, almost hesitant knock on Israel's UN Security Manager Yuri Postny's office door perked him up. Yuri called out to the chubby bio-technician, "Come in, come in. Please, sit, Gregor. I bet you are happy to be back to civilization from your African assignment, no?"

Gregor Petrov was 36, single and viewed by everyone who knew him as something of a science nerd. He was assigned to the UN's medical outreach in underdeveloped countries and was close to achieving his doctorate in bio-molecular engineering. A quiet man with thick glasses that supported his already intellectual bearing, he sat tentatively in Yuri's office side chair having no idea why he was summoned. His thinking was instinctive. From when he emigrated to Israel from Russia, it paid to be cautious. He sat stiffly, uncomfortable. He thought, *back in Russia, when security wants you, it's never a good thing.* "Is there something I can do for you, Comrade Postny?"

"First, you can knock off the comrade crap. We're in America at the UN, Gregor, and I am not KGB, for Christ's sake. You have, no doubt, guessed I have—shall we say—ties to Mossad."

"I am sorry, Yuri. Old habits die hard." Gregor began to relax, to the extent his nature would allow.

"I have an important job for you, a confidential job that requires your particular expertise." Yuri got up and closed his office door.

Gregor wondered, w*hat could he possibly want from me?* He nervously looked up from his chair and watched as Yuri returned to his own seat. *It's never good when they have to close the door.* His impatience getting the best of him, he blurted, "What could *I* possibly do for you?"

"I need you to pose as a bio-scientist and to inspect a paper. . .a formula. All I want you to do is look at it and make brief comments that would pass for an expert review. Then you will nod affirmatively to me and leave it at that." Yuri explained the exercise in detail and ended with his major selling point.

"Gregor, help me pull this off and you will be helping me save a young man's life. We'll also help our American friends put a nasty international criminal out of business."

Relieved, now that he knew what this was about, Gregor joked, "You mean I can act like I know what I am talking about?"

The wisecrack didn't work on Yuri, "No. You need to be *convincing* that you know what you are talking about."

"I will do my best, comr. . ., sorry, Yuri Postnyovich." His expression was apologetic.

"Come to think of it, when the time comes, you can slip a 'comrade' or two into the conversation for added flavor." Yuri chuckled. *Avi would love that.*

Detective Cheryl Wilson walked into the 17th precinct station house in New York City and "tinned" the desk sergeant. He inspected her badge closely and raised his eyebrows. She was shuttled through the bureaucracy and passed from one office to the other until she landed in front of Lieutenant Josh Ornath. Over his basement office door was printed, "Special Services."

"Lieutenant Ornath, I am here on the orders of Major Hawkins of the NJ State Police. We need your cooperation in a case we're running." Cheryl handed him her NJSP business card.

Lieutenant Ornath let his head drop to his chest, as he tip-toed his swivel chair around to face Cheryl. His desk was completely covered with stacks of reports. It looked like the pile on the left was trying desperately to get over to the pile on the right.

"Please tell me you're here to help me wade through this pile of administrative crap." When he finally looked up, he stared at the attractive young detective for a couple of seconds. "Uh, sorry, griping goes with the job down here in the dungeon." His attitude now more indulgent, the lieutenant asked, "What, pray tell, can I do for the State of New Jersey that I don't seem to be able to accomplish for the City of New York today?" He smiled.

"We aren't looking for help, but we need your cooperation." She filled in Ornath and finished up by saying, "We don't want to trespass on your turf without giving you a heads up. We're hoping you'll allow us to tail our subject back into New Jersey from the United Nations. We don't anticipate any activity other than tailing this guy."

In fact, Cheryl knew they could do the job without notifying NYPD, but should something untoward take place, it would be embarrassing for the state police. This way, they had the blessing of their New York counterparts.

Lieutenant Ornath grumbled, "No problem, Detective Wilson. Just don't shoot up the place, okay? Bullet holes in the UN buildings wouldn't look good." Before grudgingly swiveling back to his mountain of paperwork—and in a thick

New York accent—he added with an edge in his voice, "Hey, thanks for the courtesy call. I'll enter it into the daily log."

Cheryl left to team up with Bob Higgins. Using Mack's Motorola radios, they agreed to cruise the streets around the UN to try and identify Archer or his vehicle.

At 4:35 p.m. Bob spotted Archer's tall frame striding across First Avenue, heading for the United Nations General Assembly building. That military bearing, the crew cut and his purposeful gait stood out on New York streets like a one-man parade. Besides, Bob couldn't mistake him after his surveillances at ABP.

"Cheryl, subject approaching UN on foot. He came out of East 48th."

"Roger. I'll meet you on 48th at Second Avenue." She pulled down the "Police – Official Business" card on her visor and parked in front of a fire hydrant. Bob picked her up a few minutes later, and they slowly cruised down East 48th.

"Cheryl, his car is either in one of these parking garages or on the street."

"My bet? The street. If he needs to get out quickly, he won't want to be slowed down by driving down several stories while avoiding other cars and dealing with payment at the gate."

"Right. Let's get out and walk." Once Bob double parked, they walked down opposite sides of the street feeling for heat on the hoods of every vehicle they passed. Three were warm, but one was hot. It was a late model Dodge minivan with New Jersey plates.

"Looks good, Bob. I'll run the plate." Cheryl made a cell call to NJSP headquarters and came back with the information they were looking for.

"Stolen plate. It's gotta be him. Better call Mack." Cheryl quickly leaned over near the front fender and attached the magnetized GPS device to its underside. *There, the court order is executed.* As she raised up she saw Bob at the back of the minivan bending over for several seconds. When he came upright, he just winked at Cheryl and returned to his own van.

Mack was parked on 49th Street near 2nd Avenue. "Great job, Bob. You and Cheryl stay in the area. One of you flip around and face north on First. He has to make a left out of 48th onto First. He'll want to go directly back to Jersey and that would be west on 49th then to 11th, then up 40th and right into the Lincoln Tunnel." Mack couldn't believe their good luck. *Imagine spotting his vehicle in all this traffic, and all these one-way streets work in our favor. Go figure.*

Using their own code-speak, Bob replied, "By the way, just for backup I did a 'beam me up Scotty,' too."

"Outstanding." Mack checked his watch. *Quarter to five. Now we wait. I knew he'd be here early. Better let Kevin know it'll probably be the Lincoln Tunnel. He should be able to pick up the GPS and track him until we catch up.*

Ed Rutkowski monitored the main entrance to the cafeteria, but he could also keep an eye on the inner entrance. He and others in Whitey's crew were working at a disadvantage with no photo of Archer. There were several men who could've been Archer, but the energy wasn't right. When each was greeted by others with pleasantries and laughter, it was apparent he wasn't a business meeting and that he wasn't their man. The energy wasn't right. At almost 5 p.m., Ed figured he was in for a long evening.

Then a tall man with a short military-style haircut walked unhurried into the cafeteria. He stood at the end of the queue with his food tray and glanced around the room affecting nonchalance. But Ed knew that look: observant, cautious, expectant.

Whitey received a text from Rutkowski and joined him for a look. "That's gotta be him. Keep him in sight, we'll be set up outside. I'm farther south on First Avenue, so when you come down I can pick you up."

Whitey sent a text to a prison guard on Diego's payroll. It said, "D.G. We found our friend. Conducting business." *Gotta let the boss know we're workin' out here.*

Mack's people knew the meeting was at 7 p.m. and had identified Archer's van, but Whitey's people were literally operating in the dark. Mack's crew and Whitey's crew each stood its post waiting for something to happen, not knowing the other was nearby.

Rutkowski sat on a bench just outside the cafeteria. Calling upon his years of narcotics-surveillance techniques, he used the building's support columns to his benefit. From about 15 yards away, he kept his face hidden behind a column, resisting the impulse to look directly at Archer. He stood out of sight, but where he could still see Archer's jacket poking out from behind the column. That way he could be assured his target had not moved. As time dragged on, Ed would take a quick peek and was more and more positive he had the right guy. Archer was watching and "reading" everyone who came and went.

Rutkowski sent a text to Whitey and the others, "This has to be our guy. He's a pro. He's working the room, eyeing everybody up. I'm still good, he hasn't made me."

Mossad agent Yuri left his security office and went down to the cafeteria at 5 p.m. and took his dinner to go. Without making eye contact, he identified Archer from the photo he had received from Mack. Back at his desk, he sent a text to Avi with copies to Kevin and Mack. "The bird is on the feeder."

By quarter to seven, Mack's team was in place. Cheryl was one floor up perched in a parking garage overlooking Archer's van. Bob Higgins was on 2nd Avenue at 48th but out of sight. As is the norm, when tension mounts, some chatter takes place to ease the waiting. Cheryl radioed Bob and asked, "By the way, what was it that you were doing while I was sticking the gimmick under the van?"

"It's an old surveillance trick we used before all these electronic gizmos came along. You'll see. Just stick with us senior citizens, Cheryl. You'll learn something."

"Yeah, right!" *I might be a detective, but I hate mysteries!*

Responding to a text, Gregor stuck his head into Yuri's office and asked, "Is it time?"

Yuri waived him in. "It is, Gregor. You okay with this?"

"I am. Let's do it!"

Chapter *Forty-Four*

Archer was accustomed to long waits. During a SEAL assignment in his youth he stood without moving for nine hours in filthy water under a dock in Beirut until it was time to exfiltrate. BUD/S (Basic Underwater Demolition/ SEALS) training taught him to put his mind and body in a kind of conscious recess. He had become a very patient man.

As two men approached Archer's table, his mind transitioned from its holding pattern to evaluation mode: *The older one is the Russian I'll be dealing with. The younger is the bio-guy.*

Neither Russian had cordial attitudes. Their approach was cautious. The older one spoke first in a no-nonsense manner.

"I presume you have something for me to inspect?" His Russian accent was as thick as his bushy eyebrows.

"Possibly." Archer said, sarcastically, "After trying to bounce this meeting all over the globe, is this setting *international* enough for you?" Archer's right hand invited them to sit.

"In my experience, Americans can be reckless. We Russians have an old saying. "Beware of the goat from its front side, the horse from its back side, and the evil man from any side."

Archer nodded. "Over here we have a saying, too: 'He who hesitates is lost.'"

"Touché. I like a man who can trade barbs." The older man settled more comfortably into his chair. The younger remained quiet and nervous.

Archer kicked it off. "Here's the deal. I have something to offer you, just as you have something to offer someone else. By joining together we can avoid two transactions by selling to the same party." He smiled confidently. "Of course, there will be something in it for you, personally. Quite a bit, actually."

With measured confrontation, the older man said, "You are a bold one, aren't you? What makes you think I or my client would want to welcome such a complication when we don't need you?"

"Business is business, especially when you can make a lot more money. We're both in the same position: something to sell. You with an interested buyer, me with a similar product to sell." Archer shrugged, confidently, "Why not?" He sat back and said caustically, "You're here aren't you? You *are* interested."

"American arrogance—and perhaps some ingenuity," the older man complained yet conceded. He grinned, "Positioning is everything in a deal, isn't it?"

"So, again, why not?"

"I need to confirm the value of your goods and then we can talk about my cut. Did you bring it?"

"Of course not." There was a tense moment, then Archer laughed out loud. "But I did bring a photo of a couple of pages for you to inspect." He turned his head to the younger man and handed him his cell phone. "You must be the one to confirm my goods. Scroll two swipes to the right."

Gregor affected an intellectual pose as he studied Archer's stolen cancer formula. He took several moments before turning to Yuri and nodding his head. Gregor's halting English was heavily accented and perfectly delivered. "Is good, comrade. Is true formula for cancer drug, but with new process. Cancer cells eat other cancer cells. Become—how you say—cannibals." Tilting his head and smirking, he added conspiratorially, "And valuable, I think."

Yuri did his best to maintain a vacant expression. He chastised the younger man. "Do you have to be so enthusiastic? What kind of negotiator are you, Gregor?"

Archer's smug look put the older man on guard—or so he made it seem. "We will negotiate now that we know you have something of value." He glared at the younger man. "We will get back to you when we have spoken to our buyer. If he is interested, we can talk about the serious money you will pay us for closing a deal." He rose and the meeting was over.

On his way up the stairs, Yuri sent texts to Mack and Avi. "Done. He's coming out. All good." He winked and said, "You earned an Oscar today, Gregor."

But Gregor was puzzled. The scholarly nerd asked, "Oscar? Who is Oscar?

Yuri shook his head and walked on.

Looks like one of my old drug deals goin' down, Ed Rutkowski thought. *He meets with them. First tense, then everything changes*. He sent a text to Whitey. "For sure, some kind of deal going down here. Get ready, it's breaking up now."

Whitey spoke into his radio, "Listen up. We stick with Archer, no matter what. Got it?" Double-clicks came back in acknowledgment.

When Archer came out of the UN, Rutkowski kept him in sight but hung back in the crowd. He saw Archer walk up East 48th Street, so he positioned himself along First Avenue to see how far up Archer went. On his radio he announced, "He's walking up on a white mini-van with Jersey plates facing this way. Everybody, stay put!"

At that moment, Cheryl was providing a running commentary of Archer's movements. "Okay, guys. He's coming. He's looking around. He's at the van. Oh, shit! He just leaned over and checked the driver's side. Now he's doing the same on the passenger side. Damn!" She had to stop for a few seconds to hold her breath. "Damn," she moaned, "He found the GPS. He's sticking it on a New York Times delivery truck. Now what, guys?"

Mack radioed, "All right. It's all right, Cheryl. We knew he had good trade craft. Let's see what he does. Everybody, hang tight. Do not move."

Archer thought, *Damned Russians! Coulda figured they'd plant something on me.* He laughed out loud. "Let 'em chase the Times truck around Manhattan."

Bob, farther down the block behind Archer, radioed, "I got him, guys. I'll give you all a heads up. Let's hope he doesn't back down one-way streets tonight."

Although the meeting in the UN had not lasted long, it was now dusk and drivers were beginning to use their headlights. As Archer drove from the curb, Bob radioed, "Hey Mack, 'beam me up' is working." He threw in, "Say hello to my 'leetel' friend!"

"Right on, bro." Mack thought, *Always with the wisecracks, Bob. Now it's 'Scarface.'*

Perplexed, Cheryl asked, "What the hell are you two talking about?"

Mack smiled. "Cheryl, just so you know, Bob keeps a battery-operated drill in his van. Archer's left tail light now has a quarter-inch hole in it. In traffic at night we'll be able to spot his van among all those tail lights ahead of us by the little beam shooting out from it. Watch for 'beam me up, Scotty.'"

Cheryl laughed into her radio, "So, that's what he was doin' back there. You guys might be dinosaurs, but, damn, you are awesome!"

Chapter *Forty-Five*

Archer just made a left on First, heading for 49th."
Mack's position allowed views up and down both streets
and he had their target in his sights. "I'll let you know if he
goes straight across town or makes another turn."

Bob and Cheryl double-clicked.

"He's stopped at Second. Just sittin' there. This guy is
slick." Another half-minute passed and Archer moved. "He's
making a left onto Second. Watch for him to go around the
block looking for a tail. Stay put, kiddies!"

Bob reported, "He made a turn onto 48th Street. He's
crawling down toward First again. Yeah, he's smart. Bet he
does it again." He doubled over onto the passenger seat so
Archer couldn't spot him when he passed.

Mack's team held fast as Archer went around the block
again. Ducked down in his van, Mack radioed, "When he
rabbits, I'll let you know. Bob, you might want to go down a
parallel street, just in case." Mack gave it some more thought

and added, "And Cheryl, if you can, try to get in ahead of him on the cross-town street."

Double-clicks.

Through the chaotic traffic-clogged streets, the trio followed Archer westbound across mid-town Manhattan toward the Lincoln Tunnel. But Archer had ideas of his own.

"He's not takin' the tunnel." Cheryl cut in front of a Yellow Taxi, which earned her a middle-finger from the irate middle Eastern driver. "Looks like it's the West Side Highway, guys."

Bob was pushing his way into inching traffic on the ramp up to the West Side Highway. "I got him. Yeah, it's gonna be southbound. Shit! Get the hell outta my way, ya jerk!"

Mack was frustrated, too. "I'm jammed up. Can't see him. Got a truck in the way. Stay with him, guys. I'll catch up."

Cheryl gleefully remarked, "I can't believe it. There are at least 20 sets of taillights to my front, all moving in and out of each other's way. Can't even tell what kind of cars they are, but that little beam coming out of his left taillight screams, 'Here I am, people!' Bob, you are a genius."

"That's what Mack always calls me, right, Mack?"

Mack's laughter came through over the radio. "Yeah, in your dreams, Bob."

"See, Cheryl? He admits it: a genius in my own mind."

Whitey was glued to Bob's bumper. On his radio, he said, "This is the same guy we followed over here the other day. He is so occupied with Archer, he isn't checking his back. He's jumping all over his seat trying to make a path through for us." He chuckled, *thanks for breaking the ice jam, asshole.* But Whitey noticed something else, too. "He isn't alone, guys. He's constantly jabbering into a radio, just like us. Be aware. There must be more of them out here."

Double-clicks.

Each in their own universe of madness, the six drivers—three from each camp—scrambled to keep up with Archer heading south on the West Side Highway, through the Holland Tunnel and into Jersey City.

Mack swerved to avoid a truck changing lanes. "Idiot!" *Please, no accidents now!*

Bob reported, "We're on the magic beam, Mack. He's about six car lengths ahead surrounded by a dozen other cars. He hasn't made us, but he's practicing good counter-surveillance. He speeds up, lays back, and changes lanes often. But we're on him."

Once the craziness of New York traffic settled back to mere New Jersey pushiness, Mack advised Kevin's group of the change in plans. "We just came over the Holland and now going south into Bayonne. Better come on down, Kevin."

Double-click.

Archer thought, *Lots of traffic. No one could keep up with me in this mess. But just to be sure.* Three blocks after his planned left turn, he pulled into a 7-Eleven, parked and went inside. After a quick stop in the men's room, he stood at the window shielded by a candy kiosk and studied the traffic moving up and down Bayonne's Avenue E in both directions.

Bob radioed, "He's in a 7-Eleven here on Avenue E. I see him at the window checking everything out. He must be gettin' near wherever he's goin'. This guy is good."

"Where are you now, Bob?" Mack was still playing catch-up, but taking it easy for the moment. A local cop was cruising along behind him. *This is no time to get pulled over.*

"I'm gassing up right across the street from him in a Sunoco station. It's Avenue E near East 22nd Street. By the way, Nezzie had it cold: it had to be a ship's fog-horn on Archer's video. This area is right near the waterfront. Cheryl, is that you, a block or so back?"

Double-click.

Whitey and the special-forces twins kept up, but Philly lagged behind. "Philly, where the hell are you? We're on Avenue E. The van is gassing up across from a 7-Eleven."

"I'm getting' there, Whitey. Keep your pants dry. Behind a freakin' cop, right now. Whaddaya want me to do, pass him?"

Archer grabbed a coffee to go and got back into traffic. He retraced his route northerly and jumped a block to the south and then onto Port Terminal Boulevard. Cheryl ducked down as he went by. She radioed, "He just passed me going back up. The place must be close by. I'm gonna try something."

Cheryl jumped out of her car and flagged down the black-and-white patrol car that had been behind Mack. She ran up to the driver's side and ID'd herself to the young officer. "This is an emergency. We need your help. Now!" The young cop eyed her NJSP badge and looked around for the rest of "we." Philly slammed on his brakes to avoid hitting the police car.

Taken by surprise, the officer asked Cheryl, "What's up?"

Cheryl quickly explained she was following a suspect and climbed into the rear seat of the patrol car, directing the officer northbound on Avenue E.

The officer said, "Okay, but I have to report in. You can't just jump into my car and take over." He reached for his microphone.

Cheryl shot back, "Don't do that! Listen, I don't have time to lay it all out for you. We don't need more cops here. A kid's life is in danger and you and your car are what I need right now! Got it?"

The intensity of Cheryl's demand brought the young officer around. "Okay, but I can't hold off for too long."

They followed Archer across to Prospect and then to Port Terminal Boulevard. They were barely keeping Archer's van in sight. She radioed, "Mack, I'm in a police car going east on Port Terminal heading for the waterfront."

Mack yelled, "Bob, what the hell is she doing?" But before Bob could pick up, Cheryl explained.

"There's no traffic around here and Archer is watching for a tail. We stand out like crap on a wedding cake, so I figured he wouldn't suspect a slow-moving patrol car doin' its usual cruisin' around. I'll let you know where he ends up."

"That's what I like: initiative and quick thinking. We'll hang back here. Bob, meet me in that 7-Eleven."

"Tell you what, you guy's sound like you know what you're doing," the young officer said. "I'll cruise in and out of the lots like I'm doing a normal patrol." It was just a minute into it, but he had caught on quickly. "That way he won't think anything of it and we can keep track of him at the same time." Cheryl, impressed, nodded behind her binoculars, keeping eyes on Archer's van, its shrinking image on its way to the waterfront area.

Whitey came to a stop near the front door of the 7-Eleven and radioed his crew. "Now they're meeting up in a 7-Eleven across from a Sunoco. Stay where you are. I'll check it out." Bob and Mack were standing nearby between their vans looking serious and talking. Whitey overheard part of the conversation, as he walked by to enter the store.

"Jeez, I hope the kid's okay. It'd be a shame to get this close and—"

As Whitey came back through the door two minutes later he heard more snippets of conversation.

"She's spotted him going into a warehouse around the corner."

"Well, we can't just barge in on him. Gotta flush him out somehow."

Whitey sat in his van staring at the front glass of the 7-Eleven. *What to do? What to do? Damn! Diego wants Jose back safe and sound; but this has gotten way complicated?*

Mack was just about to split from Bob when a slightly-built man hesitantly walked up to them. He had a teardrop tattoo under his right eye—identified immediately by Mack and Bob as a man who had served time in prison. At first, the stranger just stood there, shifting his weight from one foot to the other. It was awkward. Finally, he said, "Um, are you guys familiar with the saying, 'The enemy of my enemy is my friend?'"

Chapter *Forty-Six*

Kevin Murray, with Penny and Maria onboard, arrived at the side of the 7-Eleven. Kevin, puzzled by the gathering before him, ventured an opening comment, "Of all times for my GPS to poop out on me. Mine says we're all in the middle of the Hudson River." He gave Mack a quizzical look that said, *Who the hell are these people?*

"Kevin, these folks are trying to get to Jose, too. They're working for Diego Gomez, Jose's uncle."

"Uh-huh." Kevin raised a doubtful set of eyebrows. "Does this mean a change in plan?"

"Not really. Whitey, here, agrees to remain 'in reserve.'" With that, Mack rolled his eyes and shrugged—unconvinced himself.

Cheryl and her young cop arrived. Officer Alex Morrow said, "I really have to tell my sergeant about this. I'll keep it off the radio." He started to call on his cell when Mack intervened.

"Look, officer. Please. This will be going down in the next few hours. The more people involved, the greater the risk of harm or even death to the hostage. Please hold off for now." He bolstered his argument. "Cheryl, here, represents the state police. It's their case, so . . ."

The cop thought about it a moment. "Okay, but this is my patrol district and I'm responsible for what goes down here. I guess I can wait a little while before reporting in. I'll be around in the immediate neighborhood if you need backup." He handed Cheryl his card and added with a smile, "Here's my cell number. Call me if you need me." He winked and added, "Actually, *you* can call me anytime."

Kevin cautioned, "Assuming Archer has all the equipment I think he has, he'll have an electronic perimeter in place to warn him of anyone attempting an approach. He'll have cameras posted and maybe even boobytraps." For the benefit of the young patrolman, he warned, "Setting up a traditional hostage negotiation team with all that goes with it won't work here."

Cheryl took Mack aside and looked back toward the waterfront. "Mack, who are these guys? They tailed us here? They look like they wouldn't hesitate to . . ."

"I know, Cheryl. I'm hoping they don't do something stupid. We're stuck with them for now. It's that or have our plan be blown apart. So far, they're listening to common sense." Addressing Kevin, Mack asked, "In the meantime, is there any way we can get a closer look at the front and pin down that entrance?"

Kevin sent a drone down-river and across to near the New York side of the Hudson. He then brought it north and had it hover closer to the row of warehouses on the Jersey side. Leaning over the monitor he deliberated aloud, "The light is just enough. I don't think his cameras would be able to pick up the drone with the background clutter of the Manhattan skyline, but I don't want to get too close." Once the drone was in position, Kevin motioned to Cheryl, "You say you saw which door he went into. Take a look. Do we have it?"

Cheryl studied the video feed and asked Kevin to redirect the drone's camera a couple times before saying with the most certainty she could muster, "It's either the fourth or fifth over-head door from the north end of the building." She explained to Mack, "When we stopped along the north side, I got out and peeked around the corner. It was just in time to see the door close at the bottom. The line of sight wasn't the greatest, but, yeah, the fourth or fifth." She spoke louder to inform everyone, "There's a narrow roadway along the waterfront between the warehouse and the water. The only way we can see the door is from either end. It looks like a 10 or 12-foot drop from the edge of the road down to the water. And there's no barrier."

Mack called his old friend, Chief Bill Worten at home. He explained their situation and got to the point of his call. "I know you're not in Hudson County, but could you come up with a schematic of a warehouse on the Bayonne waterfront if I give you its coordinates? Can you get someone over there to help out?"

"Why don't you just ask me for the key to the crown jewels?"

"Hey, I know it's getting late, Bill. But we're really up against it here. It's do or die time. Please try."

Whitey and Ed Rutkowski were standing off to the side, leaning against the outside wall of the 7-Eleven and taking in all of the discussions. Whitey was getting antsy. He whispered, "This is bullshit! I don't think they have a plan. We need to go in and get the kid out now."

Rutkowski replied, "I don't know, Whitey. These guys at least seem to be organized. They're goin' about it in the right way. You don't just barge in. That's a good way to lose a hostage."

"You and your cop crap. I still say all this standing around talking isn't getting us anywhere."

"What would Diego say if he was here, Whitey?" Ed knew bringing up Diego would temper Whitey's impatience. He knew if Whitey screwed this up—and Jose died—there would be hell to pay.

It worked. Whitey gazed down Port Terminal Boulevard toward the waterfront. "Yeah, well. We'll see."

Hours went by. Bob checked his watch. "Mack, it's a little after midnight. I would bet Archer is getting some shuteye, ya think?"

"So?"

"Well, what about a sneak-peek? We could go along the backside of . . ."

Mack cut him off. "We can't Bob. According to Kevin— and considering Archer's electronic background and expertise—he probably has the whole place covered. There could even be boobytraps, for all we know. No, we're gonna have to figure a way to lure him out of there, so we can go in and get the kid."

Whitey and the two specs eye-balled each other. To Bob it appeared to be a signal. He gave a heads-up to Cheryl.

The two specs and Whitey met in the dark behind the 7-Eleven. "We can do it, Whitey. It's what we were trained for. You need recon, here. Gotta know what you're up against, right? We can do a 'snoop and poop' and he'll never know we were there."

Cheryl stood near the corner of the building listening, waiting for the right moment to cut in. Finally, she stepped from around the corner and said, "Knock it off! Now, I'm giving you an order and you better not interfere with it. This is a police matter not a rodeo. You will do as you're told or I'll call that Bayonne cop back and throw all your asses in jail!"

Taken by surprise, the two specs tightened up their posture, their machismo challenged by Cheryl. Whitey's patience was at an end. He said, "I don't know about the rest of you, but I'm for some action here." To Cheryl, he said, "I know you're a state cop, but we're not gonna sit around here doin' nothing. We've got to get the kid out!" He took a step forward.

The inevitable confrontation had arrived. Mack, Bob and Kevin fell in behind Cheryl while Rutkowski and Philly lined up with Whitey and the specs. For a moment the tense standoff looked like it could turn ugly.

Mack broke the tension. "You wanna go in there? Go ahead. You, special forces guys, got your metal detectors? Got a bomb dog with ya? Got your night-vision headsets? Got all that U.S. Army good stuff with ya? Huh? No, you don't." He let that sink in. "Stupid bravado ain't gonna cut it tonight. Archer was a SEAL before he was a DEA agent. He served all over the world. He's a trained stone-cold killer, not some yahoo from the streets. You get the kid killed, you'll be next." Mack searched each of their faces.

The two specs locked eyes, taking in Mack's every word. One chewed on his lower lip. Mack drove the message home, "You think you're just gonna walk in on him? You can't be that stupid."

That ended the near skirmish and reinforced Mack's leadership over both camps. The standoff seemed to be over. Whitey wasn't happy, but without backup from his own, he had no choice. They all settled in for the night. When daylight peeked through the Manhattan skyline, a round of fresh coffee and donuts motivated limbs stiff from taking turns napping in the vehicles.

Mack decided to split them up. Bob Higgins took over the group that left the 7-Eleven area and went to the opposite side of the warehouse where Cheryl had seen the door go down. He took the two specs and Cheryl, while Mack and Kevin, along with Whitey, Philly and Rutkowski remained at the 7-Eleven. Penny and Maria sat waiting in Kevin's car.

Outwardly, Mack rationalized, "This way we have the place completely covered." To himself, he said, *dividing them allows for more control and less chance for a dumb-ass mistake. And I need to keep a close eye on Whitey.*

At 8:30 a.m. Chief Worten called with the information they needed. "It took some doing but sometimes you make your own luck. I found a retired Bayonne cop who dug up the warehouse schematic in the building department. How do I get it over to you? It's impossible to read on an iPhone."

"Bill, you are such a star. Hang on, I'm going to get a fax number at the 7-Elven we're at."

The drawing was dated June 1942 and showed World War II Liberty Ship dockage along the waterfront. Comparison with the more modern-day Google Earth depiction gave Mack confidence that the schematic was fairly accurate.

They could work with it.

Chapter *Forty-Seven*

Coming up with something that would trigger Archer to come out, but without guns-a-blazing was the challenge. The solution came about when Kevin called Yuri at the UN.

"We need to pull Archer out of his hole without endangering the hostage. How did you leave it with him? Can you message him that another meet is required?"

Yuri pondered the questions. "What if I tell him the buyer is in a hurry and we have to finalize the deal today or it's off? That might pressure him to act."

Mack was listening on speaker. "Do it. That's good. That's our only option. It's the only legitimate outside contact he would fall for. Hey, money talks, bullshit walks, right?"

Archer fed Jose another hamburger he reheated on the hot plate. He checked the cameras and went up on the roof to do his daily calisthenics. His iPhone buzzed. It was another email from the Russians. *This looks like crunch time*. Back downstairs, he punched in the phone number of his Diego Gomez contact, a private investigator named, "Mack" Mackey.

Mack looked at the iPhone and raised his eyebrows and said, "What the . . ." *This should be interesting*. He swiped on and started in aggressively. "So, you've got the kid and you want to deal. How are we gonna do this, dirt bag?" He walked around to the back of the 7-Eleven for privacy and better concentration.

"I wouldn't push my luck, P.I. You aren't in any position to make nasty remarks. Here's what I want you to tell that drug-dealing piece of shit. He lays off me and he gets little Jose back. If he or his friends ever show up in my life again, I'll come back and kill Jose, Maria and anybody else he cares about. You know I can and I'd do it, P.I. Tell him!"

"That's way too weird, Archer. Neither of you are particularly known for keeping up his end of a bargain. How would either of you know the other wouldn't break the deal? You know, you've pissed off a very dangerous man. You stole his nephew and now you want him to forget about it? I don't think so." Mack wanted to make this conversation as real for Archer as possible.

"Look. It's not complicated. If all he has to do is nothing, and he gets Jose back, what's the problem? Gomez and I understand each other. I won't poke him as long as he abides by the deal. He'll get it.

"It's your ass, not mine, Archer. I'll run it by him and get back to you."

"Take your time, P.I. I got business to attend to today."

"Just keep the kid safe, asshole. That's all I have to say." Click. Mack hung up on him.

Mack spoke into his radio, but also aloud to those standing nearby, "Listen up, everybody. I just got off the phone with Archer. As far as he knows, I'm on my way to negotiate a deal with Jose's Uncle Diego in Rahway prison. Apparently, Yuri got through to Archer. He said, 'I got business to attend to.' So, stay on your toes. He might be coming out soon."

Double-click from Bob's crew.

Jose sensed that Archer's mood had changed. Archer moved about the warehouse hurriedly. He started packing up his equipment and loading it into the minivan. Jose asked, "Are we leaving?"

"Make sure you tell your uncle how well I treated you, and tell him the next time you'll be fish food, if he comes at me again. You and your sister, too."

Archer helped Jose down the office stairs and into the back of the minivan. He took Jose by his shirt and pulled him close. "No noise. No nonsense, right?" Jose nodded.

Kevin's drone hovered over the Hudson River sending back video imagery of the warehouses along the wharf.

"An overhead door is opening. He's coming out!"

Chapter *Forty-Eight*

Bob, Cheryl, and the two specs waited word from Kevin that the door was back down before making a move. They didn't want Archer to retreat back into the warehouse once he saw them.

"Go! Go! Go!" Bob punched the accelerator and stopped short of the edge of the dock Cheryl stopping at his rear bumper. It blocked Archer's forward escape along the narrow roadway. At that same instant, Mack's and Whitey's vans rounded the corner at the other end and flew at Archer. They had him boxed in.

Mack shouted into the radio, "Remember, if you have to fire, aim high! Don't hit the kid. He might be in the back of the van."

Archer was shocked, but his survival instinct kicked in. With an iron grip, he reached back and grabbed Jose by the hair and pulled him between the seats and out the driver's door. He pressed his 9 mm Glock against Jose's throat and held him tight against his left side.

Mack lurched to a stop just 30 feet away and got out with his empty palms up, facing Archer, signaling he wasn't armed. "Ted, let the kid go. It's over. You've been set up. There is no Russian deal. There is no money. Give it up!"

One of the specs crouched down and braced himself against the corner of the building. He had the sniper rifle's crosshairs on Archer's forehead and was starting to squeeze when Bob grabbed the barrel and pushed down trying to stop the shot. It was too late. The 7.62 mm NATO round left the rifle's muzzle at 2,580 feet per second. But Bob's push against the barrel caused the round to go wide, and harmlessly puncture the left front tire of Archer's minivan.

Archer fired back in the general direction of the vehicle-blockade to his front. Just as Archer fired, Jose ducked away, dove to the concrete and wriggled under the van. Archer rushed to the back of the van but saw Whitey and Rutkowski leveling weapons in his direction. Mack yelled, "Stop firing!" They hesitated and held their weapons pointed at Archer.

Archer froze at the edge of the wharf and looked in both directions, his back to the water. Trapped. Wearing a hateful expression, he raised his automatic toward Mack.

What followed took less than a second. From only 10 yards away, Whitey and Rutkowski fired their handguns. The inexperienced Whitey missed entirely. He got off three rounds that flew past Archer. Rutkowksi, the ex-police detective, was steady. His first shot hit Archer's left shoulder. He corrected and double-tapped the Glock. Both 9 mm rounds struck Archer's mid-section propelling him backward over the edge and into the Hudson River. They heard a loud splash.

Rutkowski yelled, "I got him twice! Center mass!"

Mack ran to the edge and looked over at the murky water. Nothing. Not a ripple. Not a bubble. Just the smooth relentless flow of a river on its way back home to Mother Ocean.

When the shooting started, Kevin rushed the nurses to the scene, parking behind Cheryl's van. Jose crawled out from beneath Archer's van and was bear-hugged by Maria with tears streaming. Penny tended to a slight flesh wound suffered by one of the specs during Archer's return fire.

Mack leaned into Archer's van and located the ABP stock certificates and the secret formula in a folder under the driver's seat. But the cash Archer had taken from the company safe was gone.

Kevin crawled into the cargo area of the van to check out Archer's collection of electronic goodies and was excited by what he found. He shouted, "Mack, with all this stuff, he would've spotted us coming from at least a quarter of a mile away."

Mack signaled for Whitey and his crew to follow him. Near Whitey's van, Mack purposely stared at Ed Rutkowski. "If it weren't for the fact you likely saved my bacon, I wouldn't be saying this. This place is gonna be crawlin' with law enforcement soon." He peeked into the driver's window of Whitey's van. Sarcastically, he continued, "Unless you have permits for all this weaponry—along with receipts —I suggest you beat it the hell outta here." To Whitey, he said, "You can tell Diego that Archer is floating somewhere downstream and headin' out to sea. He'll like that, almost as much as knowing that Jose is safe and sound."

Whitey and Mack shook hands and that was that. As they backed down the wharf, Ed Rutkowski—in the front seat of Whitey's van—locked eyes with Mack. They both nodded knowingly. Mack thought, *He's been here before. He knows what a real shooting is: when death is only a trigger squeeze away, fate will have its way. Either way, actually.* Mack reflected, *too bad, he coulda been a good cop.*

Cheryl called Officer Morrow who showed up five minutes later with a patrol sergeant and four other patrol cars. The sergeant set up search and recovery assignments—one went to the north, but most searched south of the scene—looking for any sign of Archer.

The sergeant said, "He wouldn't be to the north, but I have to check anyway. The flow is north to south, so I'm sure the body will be down that way." He radioed Bayonne Police Headquarters requesting the marine unit and divers.

The stress and tension of the moment beginning to ease, Mack and Bob walked together along the waterfront. Bob checked his watch and said, "Strange. We should've found him by now. He was hit hard. It spun him around and out at least four or five feet over the water."

Mack answered, "Yeah, but something troubles me. With all that weaponry and carefully considered inventory, can you think of anything else he should've had that we didn't find in the van?"

Bob blinked a couple of times. "What if he had a . . ."

Mack blurted out, "Bulletproof vest? I can't believe he didn't have one." Mack had a disconcerting thought. He stopped and turned Bob around by the elbow. "What if he's still alive?"

Bob stared down at the dark flowing water. "Yeah, well, he *was* a Navy SEAL."

Mack leaned over to the edge and yelled down into the water, "Archer, you bastard! Are you still with us?"

Three days later, Mack's office phone rang. Nezzie was at lunch, so Mack picked up. The Bayonne detective reported they learned that when Archer rented the warehouse, he also rented a small garage farther north. When they executed a search warrant, they found it empty.

"Well, not entirely empty," the detective advised. "There were bloody bandages, an old Navy sea bag and a strong odor of urethane and enamel—probably what you would paint a car with. The car wasn't there, though. The landlord said the guy had a fancy car when he rented him the space, an Infiniti."

Mack called Bob and conferenced in Kevin Murray. "Guys, looks like we were right. Archer's in the wind. We know he was wounded, but it couldn't have been bad enough to stop him. The slime ball painted the Infiniti and took off in it."

Bob said, "This is too incredible. Too freakin' weird. I was just about to call you, Mack. Cheryl just called: Diego Gomez was being transferred to federal prison to await deportation when the bus he was in over-turned and went down an embankment on the New Jersey Turnpike. Both U.S. Marshals were knocked unconscious. They said the bus was cut off by a truck and that's the last they saw of Gomez."

"He was busted out? Really? This craziness just won't stop. Unbelievable!"

"I know. It's nuts."

Kevin said, "It's too much. Can you believe this? Archer and Gomez out there at the same time. Which one would you put your money on?"

"Now, that's a tough one, Kevin!"

Chapter *Forty-Nine*

Six months later

The hotel clerk lightly tapped the bell. "Please sign the register, Mr. Bledsoe." And, just loud enough for the bell boy to hear, he said, "Front!"

Bledsoe's suite was spacious and elegant. After all, it was the Four Seasons. Los Angeles was delightful this time of year. Cool mornings and pleasant warm breezes throughout the day. He slid back the window, took a Coke from the minibar, kicked off his shoes and stretched out on the king-size bed.

"What the hell. I've got an hour before he gets here." He drifted off.

The phone rang. "Mr. Bledsoe, there's a Mr. Vaughn here in the lobby. He says he has an appointment with you. May I send him up?"

Bledsoe held the door open for the tall, thin businessman. He was dressed impeccably in a gray three-piece suit. "Come in Mr. Vaughn. May I fix you a drink?"

"No, thanks." There was an awkward moment. Vaughn didn't know whether to sit or stand or what to do next. He was nervous.

"Please, sit down." Bledsoe led him to the table at the other end of the room near the opened sliding window. The curtain had a steady, slight billow to it.

Bledsoe smiled and waited for Vaughn to speak.

Finally, after an uncomfortable pause, Vaughn said, "You'll have to forgive me Mr. Bledsoe. This is all new to me."

"I understand. Why don't you just give me some of the history and work your way up to the main point of your visit?"

For the next half hour, Vaughn related his company's problem with a competitor. Bledsoe listened patiently.

His presentation finished, Vaughn seemed more at ease. He asked, "So, Mr. Bledsoe, just exactly what is it that you can do for me?"

His response was automatic, but his penetrating stare was uncomfortably emphatic. His left shoulder was a little stiff, but he leaned forward anyway and said forcefully, "I get things fixed, Mr. Vaughn. I fix things." His penetrating eyes glued to Vaughn's, he added, "Whatever it takes!"

East Los Angeles—or "East Los" as the locals christened it—has been the heart of the Latin community since California was carved out of Mexico. Twenty-eight-year old Enrique Romo was leader of el Pachucos, a gang of Mexican youths whose income was derived from dealing crack in Los Angeles and neighboring cities. Romo kept his finger on the pulse of the city by virtue of a network of cooks, waiters, bell boys, cab drivers, and landscapers. They respected and feared him. They cooperated—or else.

Enrique remarked to his driver, "This phone call should be profitable." Normally, discussions between two drug gangs don't go well. This was the exception. In deference to the older drug dealer on the other end, he chose his words carefully.

"I believe we have located your package Señor Gomez."

"Are you sure, Enrique? There have to be many tall gringos in East Los."

"Si, jefe. This is true. But this one matches the photograph perfectly. He has the short flat haircut and walks with confidence. And here is the best part: Such nice wheels! It is a beautiful tan colored Infiniti. Except for the color, is that not the car you described?"

"Which hotel did you say?"

"Only the best. The Four Seasons, Beverly Hills. Oh, and did I say his room number? It is 1535 on the top floor."

"Gracias, amigo. I will be there by sundown. Please keep him company for me."

"We are, jefe. I have a man on a rooftop nearby looking right into his room.

"Excellent."

"You owe me, Jefe."

"Yes, I do, Enrique."

In Room 1535, discussion had finally gotten around to finances. Bledsoe said, "Mr. Vaughn, these assignments are not without risks. I will have expenses. My usual upfront retainer is $50,000, then when I see what's required we agree to a final figure. Understand?"

Vaughn was unfazed by the amount. "This is important. We are prepared to pay your price, whatever, if you can do what you say you can do. How do we close the deal?"

The knock at the door was subtle, just what would be expected at the Four Seasons. Bledsoe rose, looked at Vaughn and smiled, "Expecting someone?"

He peeked through the eye-hole in the door and saw a hotel waiter holding a small hors d'oeuvres tray. The waiter announced, "Compliments of the house, Mr. Bledsoe."

Bledsoe looked back at Vaughn and commented, "Whaddaya know, perfect timing. A great way to celebrate our business." He reached over and unlocked the door.

The Los Angeles SWAT team was efficient. They burst into the room and put both Bledsoe and Vaughn on the floor facedown before either could inhale a shocked breath.

The team leader—a tough sergeant with a wizened face—leaned down close to Bledsoe and sarcastically said, "Mr. Theodore Archer, I presume?"

Wild-eyed and shaken, Mr. Vaughn scuffed his chin on the carpeting as he turned his head. "Archer? Who's Archer? You guys must have the wrong room!" He shouted, "Get your knee out of my back. You're hurting me. Do you know who I am?"

Archer, shaken, heard a voice from behind and above. "It was the Infiniti, Archer. You shoulda switched cars. Hard to give it up, huh?" The plainclothes detective leaned against the doorway looking casually down at his grimacing captive.

The detective unraveled a piece of chewing gum. "Want a piece, Ted?"

Archer strained against the handcuffs to look back and up. "Fuck you!"

The detective leaned down and held the arrest warrant and detainer in Archer's face. It was for the murder of Dr. Peter McGinn. The detective said, "Shame on you. Leaving fingerprints at the scene of a crime. Very careless."

"But jefe, we would have an excellent shot at your man as the police take him from the hotel. The police cars are all waiting at the loading dock in the back. Our man is in position."

"No! Don't do that. I thank you for your services, Enrique. I will handle it from here." He continued solicitously, "Let me know if I can ever do something for you."

Enrique said, "Of course, Jefe. We never know, someday I may call on you. Adios, Señor Gomez." Enrique stared at his phone and thought, *that day will never come. Lay down with the dog, accept the fleas.*

Diego Gomez sat quietly at a small corner table in Tijuana's Blue Moon Cafe, tasting salt on the rim of his second margarita. *I couldn't have dreamed this up. Archer on the inside and me out here. Looks like I have him on ice this time.* The thought caused him to almost choke on his drink. He sputtered, "On *ICE*. Oh, yeah, Five-0 would fuckin' love that one!"

Chapter *Fifty*

Sandwiched between two hefty plainclothes New Jersey State Troopers, a hand-cuffed and ankle-shackled Ted Archer inched his way down each step of the American Airlines flight from Los Angeles. Instead of disembarking through the customary jetway and through Newark Liberty International's terminal, arrangements were made to meet the flight at ground level.

The officers guided slow-shuffling Archer across the tarmac, through the back of the baggage area and into a supervisor's side office. The first familiar faces Archer saw were those of Mack and Bob. Archer's sardonic smile said it all. He spoke first. "I knew it had to be you guys. You never give up, do you?"

Mack said, "We're not here to gloat, Ted. Well, maybe a little. But we want to bring you up to date. Like I said when we last met along the Hudson, you'd been had with that Russian secret formula deal. We set that up to find you. The rest was just good tradecraft."

"Humph. So, tell me this, asshole, how the hell did you follow me from the UN in all that traffic? I know I got rid of the GPS gimmick and I watched for a tail."

Mack and Bob grinned. Bob said, "That'll remain *our* secret."

Mack followed up, "After the 'Shootout-on-the-Hudson,' the Bayonne PD went to the Basking Ridge PD and the Somerset County Prosecutor's Office. Given your connection to McGinn, they took his death very seriously and, lo and behold, your fingerprint turned up on the garage door opener. Bad mistake. You were sloppy, Ted."

Archer's words were almost a whisper. "So I was told. It only takes one, doesn't it, P.I.?"

"Oh, I almost forgot. We were able to find and interpret the program in your laptop that took over Henry Lott's car and caused that non-accident. Shame on you, again, Ted. Using 'Infiniti' as your password. I was giving you way too much credit." Mack added, "So, there's one more murder charge comin' your way."

Mack paused a moment, then said, "There's a deep absurdity in all of this. You remember our meeting in Wendy's condo that night? Remember my warning? All you had to do was hit the road and you'd have gotten away scot-free." Mack slowly shook his head side to side. "But no, you thought you were smarter than everyone else. In the end, it was your own arrogance that did you in, Ted."

He simply stared at his cuffs. Archer had no response. His face said it all.

Bob Higgins couldn't resist one last dig. "Ted. I'm sure you remember Diego Gomez, your other close friend? Well, he bugged out on the U.S. Marshals during a road-trip." Bob moved closer to Archer, tilting his head to one side and whispered, "It'll be his turn to *stick it to you* on the inside. Hell, he's probably downing tequilas somewhere out of everyone's reach. And I bet right now he's working on his "Dead Ted' plan." Bob ended with, "You've run your string, Archer. You're done."

As they left, Mack threw over his shoulder, "Watch yourself in there, Ted. They don't allow bullet-proof – *or shank-proof*— vests where you're headed."

Driving West on Interstate 78, Bob said with a satisfied grin, "Mack, you had it right. When things line up right, guys like Archer *do* get it in the end."

THE END

"ACCIDENTAL P.I."

A Private Investigator's Fifty-year Search for the Facts

A Memoir by David B. Watts

Have you ever wondered what it would be like to be a real-life private investigator watching the bad guys through binoculars during a surveillance or interviewing witnesses in a murder investigation? Or, how about seeing yourself testifying in a big federal court case? Maybe you could envision yourself conducting a corporate corruption investigation for some of the Fortune 500 companies. Your author, David B. Watts, has done all of those things and is pleased to share many of them with you in his first book, Accidental P.I., also published by North Loop books.

As a real-life private investigator, David's life story treats you to these experiences and more. Unlike P.I. work as portrayed in the movies and on television, Accidental P.I. offers a peek behind-the-scenes showing how investigators really get the job done.

New York Times best-selling author, Randy Wayne White, says, "I thoroughly enjoyed Accidental P.I. by David B. Watts. It is a series of tales that are all-the-more compelling because they are fact, not fiction, although Watts writes with the skill of a novelist."

Accidental P.I. is available at Barnes & Noble, Amazon.com, eBooks, and by contacting the author directly at his website: www.davidbwatts.com.

Spring 2016

"LOOSE ENDS"

Murder in the New Jersey Suburbs

A Novel by

David B. Watts

What starts out as a relatively low-level crime... insurance fraud... evolves quickly into a triple murder case in the up-scale community of Summit, New Jersey. A wealthy lawyer-turned politician is charged with brutally killing his socialite wife, while the real perpetrator goes on a killing spree to cover his crimes. The tension builds, as the defense team cannot seem to get over its internal wrangling. An ambitious, young, assistant-prosecutor steps over the line ethically in her eagerness to convict the defendant. A corrupt U.S. Congressman pulls strings in the background, and all the while the cunning killer, a psychopathic genius, does his share of devious meddling with the justice system.

Private Investigator "Mack" Mackey and his side-kick, Bob Higgins, struggle with the slim set of facts they have to go on. Will the good guys win in the end? Will our client be exonerated? Maybe, but not after a crazy gallop through the halls of justice and a lot of head-scratching sessions with no shortage of bad-tempered outbursts. The story builds to a last-minute court room blockbuster ending.

With its twists and turns and realistic dialogue, "Loose Ends" is a cliff-hanger that seizes the reader's curiosity. What can possibly happen next! As the story develops, readers will wonder how in the world this tale can unwind and justice be served in the end. Author David B. Watts has drawn upon his many years as a private investigator to entertain his readers with a tale of depraved murder and perversion of the justice system. A fun read!

Available at Barnes & Noble, Amazon.com, eBooks, and by contacting the author directly at his website: www.davidbwatts.com.

Fall 2017

About the Author

David B. Watts, a licensed private investigator for the past four decades, specializes in fraud and business investigations. He and Linda, his wife of 56 years, worked for major law firms, insurance companies and the Fortune 500 in the busy New York to Philadelphia corridor on cases ranging from kickbacks to special security issues. He has also worked several murder cases and thousands of insurance fraud matters.

Dave's investigation career began in his twenties as a Plainfield, New Jersey patrolman. He was promoted to detective, then joined the Union County Prosecutor's Office as a county investigator. These early experiences eventually launched him into a lifetime of investigation work in private sector investigation work. His pursuit of the facts brought him into state and federal courts as well as the board rooms of major corporations. Respected by his peers, Dave continues to take on special investigations, now in his seventies.

Authenticity comes through in his writing after a lifetime of experience, and he shares that with his readers. Who'd be better to portray the real ins and outs of private investigations in a novel? Go to Dave's website: www.davidbwatts.com for more information or to contact him.

CPSIA information can be obtained
at www.ICGtesting.com
Printed in the USA
LVHW051055150419
614196LV00014B/304